How I got hooked up with Jimmy D. Watley:

"Just walk on in and look for a man named Jimmy D. You'll see his name on the back of his belt, and he'll be waiting for you."

Which I did, smelling those onions and all the cigar and cigarette smoke, looking around at everybody and scared right down to the bottom of my feet.

The back wasn't crowded because it was still morning, but there were people back there and I could hear the crack of a rack of pool balls getting busted. Then I heard somebody yell a cussword real loud and somebody else start laughing. It was Jimmy D. and another man who were shooting 9-ball, a game where whoever makes the 9-ball wins, and Jimmy D. had just made the 9-ball on the break.

When Jimmy D. wasn't being a bodyguard or collecting bad debts from people, he was hustling pool, your honor, and right from the start I kind of looked on him as a hero. I think anybody would've.

Jimmy D., Sidewinder, and Me

OTTO R. SALASSI

BORZOI SPRINTERS · ALFRED A. KNOPF
New York

Dr. M. Jerry Weiss, Distinguished Service Professor of Communications at Jersey City State College, is the educational consultant for Borzoi Sprinters. A past chair of the International Reading Association President's Advisory Committee on Intellectual Freedom, he travels frequently to give workshops on the use of trade books in schools.

A BORZOI SPRINTER PUBLISHED BY ALFRED A. KNOPF, INC.

Library of Congress Catalog Card Number: 86-29508
ISBN: 0-679-80135-9
RL: 5.6

First Borzoi Sprinter edition: April 1990

Manufactured in the United States of America
1 2 3 4 5 6 7 8 9 10

FOR THE BOOJ,
AND WELL ABOUT TIME

Dear Judge Francis, your honor,

My lawyer, Mr. Harmon, says that you have taken my case under what he calls "advisement," and that means that you are trying to decide what kind of punishment I deserve. He also said that I should write my side of the story down and give it to you because it didn't get told very good at my trial. I am in my own cell and Mr. Harmon has given me lots of paper and pencils and he says that I should just tell you everything that led up to the night of the shootings. He says for me to take it one point at a time and answer all the charges that people have charged me with. Since I ain't got nothing but time, that is what I will try to do.

Charge number one, made by Mr. Broemel from the Children's Home in Vicksburg:

Mr. Broemel said that I come from what he calls "bad stock," and that I was a problem child at the home and nobody would take me in for adoption, and that I once attacked him with a knife.

That is not right.

In the first place he never knew either of my parents, and neither did anyone else know them. My father, whose name was Tobias Monk, was never in Mississippi, and got killed out west, I have learned, working on Boulder Dam.

1

My mother, Rose Monk, died of tuberculosis after she got sick on a train when I was two. They put us both in quarantine in Vicksburg, and she died without ever getting out. As far as I know, I do not have a single living relative, and so I don't know how Mr. Broemel or anybody else can say what kind of stock I come from, though I would appreciate it if they could.

As for me being unadoptable, your honor, that has never been my fault. The name my mother and father gave me is Dumas Monk, and I have no misconceptions about how I look to other people: I look like a Dumas, which is to say I'm big, gawky, dumb-looking, tow-headed, and generally misproportioned. My feet are too big for my bottom, my bottom is too big for my shoulders, my shoulders are too big for my head, and my head is too small for my ears. I make people who look at me look sad, or look worried about me, though sometimes I can do things with my face and make them smile—especially little kids.

You have seen me yourself, your honor, and know what I'm talking about. Now ask yourself, am I the kind of kid you'd want to adopt and raise as your own? Well, nobody else ever did, either. They used to come into the orphanage and look us all over, and I got to where I knew who they were going to take before they did; I got to where I could see them coming up the walk and could tell. The secret was, they took kids who looked the most like they themselves looked, and my trouble was nobody ever looked like me, or was even close.

After I figured all that out, it didn't hurt my feelings so much not to get picked. I quit getting my hopes up, but that doesn't mean I made myself unadoptable.

In a lot of ways, the way I look has been fun and useful. Take my feet, for instance. They are so big that I can stand up straight, with my arms at my sides, and I can start leaning slowly forward toward somebody who's talking to me and they won't know what's happening but they'll know something is wrong, and they'll start leaning back, and pretty soon they'll lose their balance. I can lean left and right and back and forth and every which way and make people dizzy and start laughing.

That is why I was not a problem like Mr. Broemel said I was. I was the oldest kid in the home, 14, and had been there the longest, more than 10 years, and I took care of all the other kids like big brothers do. I was the one they came to when they couldn't sleep, when they were scared, or missed their mamas and daddies, not Mr. Broemel or his fat, ugly wife. All the Broemels ever cared about was themselves and the stuff they stole that was supposed to go to us.

One Christmas, for instance, a big box of clothes came over from the Salvation Army. I helped unload it in Mr. Broemel's office, and right on top was a brand-new flannel shirt that somebody hadn't wanted. I needed a shirt and it was my size, but it was Mr. Broemel's size too, so guess who got it?

I can tell you exactly when that shirt came in, but I have to work backwards: on this Christmas, which is 1948, I will probably be still here in jail; on last Christmas, which was 1947, I had just come here to Hot Springs, so it was the Christmas before that, 1946. The shirt was blue with black squares on it like a checkerboard, and I'll be durned if Mr. Broemel didn't have it on when he came to my trial to say how rotten I was.

Your honor, I realize that some of the things I am going to tell you, like about that shirt, are going to sound like I'm just full of sour grapes. That's one of the things that the social worker said about me at the trial that I can't deny, that I have had such a hard life that I can't help being bitter. In some ways I admit I am, and I also admit, as a matter of fact, that I was bitter when I saw him standing up there with his hand on the Bible, wearing that shirt, and that's why I got mad and jumped up in court and called him a son of a bitch and cussed him like I did.

Now as to the second part of Mr. Broemel's charge, that I attacked him with a knife.

That is a serious charge. I can't stand Mr. Broemel at all and wouldn't care if he fell dead tomorrow, but I am not a violent person and I would never do anything to hurt him if I could help it.

What happened, starting at the beginning, was this:

It gets hot in Mississippi, a lot hotter than here in Arkansas, and when it does there ain't much you can do. People accuse Mississippians of being shiftless and lazy, but those that do have never been down there in July and seen what it can be like.

And the orphanage didn't even have a good fan, or trees around it to keep the sun off, or anything. It was just a big old two-story wooden building that had once been a county school. Downstairs on one side was an old classroom that was the playroom and dining hall; behind it was the kitchen. The entrance and stairs were in the middle of the building, and downstairs on the other side was where the Broemels lived and had an office.

Upstairs there were two big dormitories, one with 20 or 25 bunks like the kind they used in the army, and that was for the girls, and one with 20 or 30 bunks in it for the boys. Sometimes they moved the bunks around, depending on what the orphanage had the most of, boys or girls. There were bathrooms on both sides and they had water and commodes when I left, but when I first got there all there was was a pump where we pumped our own water, and four big piss pots that got filled up every night, and we had to dump them in the outhouse every morning.

In the summer, you couldn't stand to be up there. The sun beat down on the roof, and it was like being in an oven. You couldn't stand being out in the play yard either, because it was almost as hot out there. We were nine miles from town and didn't have any way to get there, and two miles at least from anywhere to swim or fish. The Big Black River was the closest place and it was good for fishing, but you wouldn't want to swim in it because of the snakes.

So what I did was take everybody down to the cellar where it was dark and full of coal dust because there was a coal bin for the furnace, and what we did down there was play our regular games. There was hopscotch, which the girls played, and jacks, which the girls also played, and things like jump rope and dolls, which the girls also played, but there wasn't much for boys. We all had knives, pocket knives and the hunting kind, because playing with knives, whittling things, carving swords, was about all we could do. And that's what we did, played games with our knives, all except mumble-peg, which we couldn't do because the floor was concrete.

And I had invented a game that was the best game ever. It was where we threw our knives at targets, which lots of kids do, but I had an obstacle course laid out, something like the kind that the army uses in basic training, where we walked through, and my targets were as good as we could make them. There was a line on the floor that you walked and places marked where you had to stop and throw from. The targets were old hunks of logs and big pieces of wood that I'd carved to look like things, or painted with some old

6

brown enamel. There was one log that looked like an alligator, so I painted teeth on it, and eyeballs, and it looked pretty good. There was a limb that I made into a snake. I had a bird, and I forget what all. One target was an old door that I'd painted with the silhouette of a gunslinger about to draw his guns. The best one was the top of an old table that I painted to look like a German soldier sitting behind the sights of a machine gun; I had swastikas on his armbands, and I'd filled some old feed sacks with coal and stacked them up to make them look like sandbags.

What we used to do was time ourselves to see how long it took to go through the course, throwing our knife and sticking it in every target and not being able to go on to the next target till we got a point-first hit, which was worth one point, or we hit and stuck, which was worth two points, or we hit and stuck in a vital organ, which was worth five.

We didn't have a stopwatch or a clock or a watch at all, and so we had to count the seconds out loud so everybody could hear. "One-one-thousand, two-one-thousand, three-one-thousand," and so on. I, of course, was the champion, and nobody could ever beat me, though from time to time I would throw bad on purpose and let one of the little kids win.

Now one of the targets was hung from the ceiling and was kind of small. It was the silhouette of what had started out to be a sniper in a palm tree, but the tree had looked like an umbrella, so I just turned it into a parachute and had a German coming down in it, armbands, swastikas, and everything.

The ceiling was kind of high, so I hung the target near the top of the stairs to the kitchen, and that was so we could get our knives back when they stuck, and so the little kids could get closer and throw from the stairs.

If you threw and stuck, you ran up the stairs, and the last target was a board on the floor that you bombed. By bombing, your honor, I mean you sighted down your blade and let the knife go as smoothly as you could, and you tried real hard to hit the target instead of the concrete. That was a problem with throwing at the parachute, too: when you missed you sometimes hurt your knife, broke the point off, or bent it good.

So what we all did was have two knives—one good one, and one we didn't care if it got broke or not. My bad knife was from the kitchen, a butter knife that I'd sharpened to a point. You couldn't break that thing if you tried.

I wanted you to know all of that so you'd know what I was doing when Mr. Broemel says I went after him.

Everybody was counting, "41-one-thousand, 42-one-thousand, 43-one-thousand . . . ," and I was trying to set a new course record. I remember it exactly because I was trying to impress a new girl in the home whose name was Becky Chaney, and I was going against a kid named Roger who was trying to impress another girl, one named Judy Malone, and I think we might've made a small bet on who was the best, something like a nickel or a dime.

Anyway, he'd gone through in something like 55 seconds, and I was working on a new world's record. I'd started like I was a big game hunter in a movie and the cameras were on me, ducking my head from the danger as I went from spot to spot, holding my hands up over my eyes like I was trying to see in the distance, showing off.

I'd just gotten to the bottom of the stairs for the last two, and was just letting go, when Mr. Broemel opened the door and started down. My butter knife hit and stuck right there beside his head, and in the meantime I had my other knife ready and raised like I was going to stab somebody, because I was still showing off, and I went charging up the stairs screaming "Bonzai," like on a suicide charge. And that's what it was all about. He walked in at the wrong time, and I must have scared him without meaning to, and he's held it against me all this time.

And against all the others, too. Even though he knew we were just playing a game, he took up all the knives and never gave them back, and there wasn't anything to do after that at all.

The cell they've got me in is OK, but it doesn't have any lights, just the light from the hall, which isn't good enough to see by, so I have to stop writing now. That's all I have to say about Mr. Broemel, anyway, except some of the kids that were there that day I was supposed to have attacked him might still be there in the home, or they might be easy to trace—Becky Chaney, or Roger Koetter, or Judy Malone. They'll tell you what really happened.

Charge number two, made by Mr. George Barber, who is the Warren County Juvenile Officer in Vicksburg:

Mr. George Barber wrote to say that since I violated the terms of an agreement I made with the Rhodus family and the State of Mississippi, I am in violation of the law and am officially wanted by the state as being a fugitive from justice, for being a juvenile delinquent, for truancy, and for not having any occupation or means of support.

To answer those charges, which I am not denying, I have to tell you what happened. First of all, about getting placed with the Rhoduses:

It wasn't but a week after the incident in the cellar, when I was looking out the front window and I saw Mr. Barber come walking up the walk with these two big country-hick-looking goons, and I knew it was for me that they were coming.

Sure enough, it wasn't five minutes before Becky, Roger, and Judy-booty came running upstairs to get me. I'd already thought about trying to skip out the back, because I knew it wasn't going to be good, but that wouldn't work cause I didn't have a whole quarter to my name, or anywhere to go, or anything.

Everybody knew who Mr. Barber was. He was the person who brought kids to the home and arranged for them to get put somewhere, either in a foster family or in the state school in Bolton. Every year he had to write a report to Jackson about our welfare, and talk about stretching the truth. . . .

I went down to the office and he was in there with Mr. Broemel and the two men, who looked as big and mean up close as they did coming up the walk. Their names were Roy and Thurman Rhodus, and they were brothers and partners in something called the Rhodus Brothers' Hauling and Delivery.

They were dressed like for church, but you could tell they hadn't been to church in their lives. They wore starched clean white shirts that didn't fit. Roy was tall and skinny, and his shirt collar was so big you could have stuck an apple down it. Thurman was over six feet and had a gigantic beer belly, and his collar was so tight it looked like his head was going to pop. Both of them had shaved their faces too close to be comfortable, and they'd tied the knots in their ties so tight they were going to have to be cut apart with scissors. Roy was wearing khaki pants and Thurman was wearing bib overalls; they were both wearing tight black military surplus shoes that had never been worn before. The leather bottoms of the shoes hadn't been marked up except by the walk from the truck to the chairs they were sitting in.

It was going to be what I had figured it was, and Mr. Broemel had papers for me to sign and take with me.

"This one says you are in good health, have had all your shots, have been to the dentist and have good teeth." I signed it.

"This one says you've been to school, can read and write at the ninth grade level, and have had the required courses in Mississippi history and citizenship." I signed it, too.

11

"This one is a copy of the court order that placed you in the county home, and with it is an official death certificate for your mother and an official letter from the state of Nevada verifying your father's death." Those three weren't for me to sign but just take with me.

"This last one is your information sheet. It gives the cemetery and grave number where your mother is buried and other information, like where and when you were born. It also lists the possessions your mother had with her when she died. . . ."

And he gave me a woman's purse that had some stuff in it. It was woman's stuff, mostly—bobby pins, a hairbrush, lipstick, and things like that. But there were two things that were important and that come up again. One was a playing card, an ace of spades, which must have meant something to her, and the other was a locket that had a little picture of her and my father together. The picture was too little and too blurry to tell much about them, but it looked like my father had a mustache.

If you want to know how good a detective I am, I know that my mother's hair was red because there was red hair in her hairbrush, and my own hair sometimes looks red, especially in the summer.

I remember things, too, like what Mr. Barber said next. He said first that I wasn't getting adopted, but placed in a foster home because I was getting too old and getting to be too much trouble to stay where I was, and that it was time for me to start learning how to make my way in the world. This was the agreement: "The Rhodus family runs a hauling and delivery business, so you're going to work for them. They'll give you a place to sleep, feed you, and pay you 10 dollars a week every Friday afternoon out of the money the state pays them. In return you have to work and they have to be satisfied with what you do."

"What about school?" I wanted to know. I was supposed to be going into the tenth grade. I didn't especially like school, but I didn't dislike it, either, and it was going to be easier, I had the feeling, than working for the Rhoduses.

"The law says you've got to go to school till you're 16, but the school has a special program where you get credit for working. It's called Diversified Occupations or D.O.," he said, and according to him there were about 20 kids in school in it. I have never heard of a law yet that there is no way to get around.

My mind was already planning things. At 10 dollars a week, I figured I could save my money, and when I got enough saved, and when I had figured everything out, *then* I could make my getaway, but he warned me about that next.

"The law also says that you have to mind what the Rhoduses tell you to do, and they've got the right to punish you if you don't. You're 14 now, and you've got three years, till you're 17, before you're legally free to do what you want. When you're old enough, you can leave and get another job, or join the army, which the boy they have right now is doing, or you can leave the state. Till then you've got to stay where you're put." Then came the good part:

"If you don't, and if the Rhoduses don't want to keep you, you won't come back here. You'll go to Bolton, and I guarantee you won't like it there. There's murderers in there, and sex and dope fiends, and torture and solitary confinement."

And that, your honor, was what the law let them do to me; when Mr. Barber says I broke the law by running away, that was the law I was breaking. I had to do what the

13

Rhodus brothers told me to do, or else they would beat me till I did, and I had to keep doing it till I was 17 or else they could have me sent to prison.

Judge Francis, your honor, if that wasn't the same as slavery, what else could you call it?

Mr. Harmon, my lawyer, just came by and read what I've written so far and says I'm doing fine. I hope so, and I hope I haven't said anything to make you mad at me, your honor.

Mr. Harmon also says that this is not the time to be bashful or squeamish about telling the truth, as I have already been found guilty. He says that the "Great Day of Judgment" is coming for everybody, and that it's just coming a little early for me.

So here I go again:

I have told you about the law I broke, now let me tell you about Mr. Barber's charge, that I broke the agreement I made with the Rhoduses, that I didn't like to work, and that I started gambling and hanging out at the pool hall all the time.

That's not completely true, either.

I had five minutes to get my stuff together and meet the Rhodus brothers outside. Up at my bunk I got to take my blankets and sheets and pillow because whoever got my bed would get all new stuff except a mattress. I rolled all my clothes up in the bedding like a bedroll and tied it all with shoestrings. I had some things I wanted to give away, and there were kids who wanted them—stuff I'd carved, a yoyo, a harmonica that sounded bad. I had another knife, one that Mr. Broemel didn't know about, and I took that. I also had an old copy of *Gray's Anatomy*, which wasn't any good because all the good pictures of girls and women had been torn out long before I got it, but I gave it away to the girls, anyway, because it still had some pretty good ones of boys.

Becky wanted to kiss me, but I wouldn't let her, not in front of everybody. Kissing her was dangerous because she'd seen a love scene in a movie where Dorothy Lamour or Hedy Lamarr "swooned from the rapture of the moment" (as she called it) and so lately, when she kissed you, you had to grab her to keep her from falling and breaking her neck.

It didn't take five minutes.

Downstairs, and 12 years of my life were over. I got in the Rhoduses' old truck and we drove away, and I never saw the children's home, or any of the kids, or my childhood playing grounds again.

I was in the middle of the seat of a pickup truck and I had to hold my feet up because the thing didn't have a floorboard. It had all rusted out, and you could see the road moving underneath when you looked straight down. It was a good thing, too, because the Rhodus brothers dipped tobacco and could spit straight down instead of out the windows. Spitting out the windows will sometimes blow back in on you.

But we didn't get very far before they stopped. We barely got out of sight of the home when Roy, who was driving, pulled over, and they both got out and peed right there in the road. Then they crawled up in the back and started changing clothes. They pulled off their new shoes and put on boots; Roy's were cowboy and Thurman's were greasy mechanic's. They also took off their white shirts and ties and put on their regular clothes. Roy wore a fancy cowboy shirt with pearl buttons, and Thurman wore a dark blue welder's. Right there in the road they opened cans of beer and started drinking them, and I had to sit in back to give them more room.

The truck was a real dilly, with so many coats of paint on it and so many dents and rust holes in it that it was hard to tell what color it was supposed to be. Two things in it worked perfect, though, the engine and the radio.

I'd say, just offhand, that that truck could do well over 100 miles an hour if you had a straight road and no cops around. They kept it looking bad on purpose, I always figured, for reasons all their own.

The radio, I'd say, had a speaker you could hear in the next county, and they weren't afraid of turning it up. It had to go pretty loud to get over the engine noise that came up from the floorboard that was missing. What was worse, though, was they both liked to sing. They knew the words to every song on the radio, which wasn't unusual as everybody, I think, does. But not everybody could sing that loud or that bad.

One of the songs that was real popular that summer was a tearjerker called "I'll Dance at Your Wedding," and you should have heard them singing along to that. When we got into town the one they were doing was about being happy in my blue heaven. That was the name of it, "My Blue Heaven." People were looking at us and it was embarrassing.

To feed me and give me a place to sleep, that was their part of the bargain. Since it wasn't morning but late afternoon when they came to get me at the home, I figured they were taking me to their home to do just that. It wouldn't be long before I needed a place to sleep, and I needed something to eat as soon as I could get it. I had missed supper and my stomach was growling as loud as the radio.

Instead, they took me to their garage, which was down on North Washington, on that little strip of land between where Highway 61 starts toward Memphis, and the railroad yards.

Their place hadn't been built as a garage, but as a factory or machine shop of some kind. On the highway side there was a loading dock for trucks, and on the railroad side there was a loading dock for boxcars. The south end of the place had a big hangar-like door, and they stayed open all the time except in the dead of winter.

Inside it was like a big gym, except the floor was concrete instead of wood, and you could see where big machines had been anchored in.

There was thick, caked grease everywhere, and all along the high roof were pigeons' nests, so you were always in danger of getting bombed on. There was a bunch of trucks and buses in there leaking more grease and getting bombed on.

We drove all the way down the building, past all the trucks, and stopped in front of a desk. There were calendars everywhere with pictures of women in bathing suits doing sexy poses, the kind where you lift up a plastic cover on the outside of the picture and the bathing suit comes up. We stopped and got out of the truck and Roy said, "Well, this is it."

At first I didn't know what he meant and thought they were going to have me sleep right there in the garage, and then I saw. That's where they *all* lived, right there in the garage—him and Thurman, their Ma, who everybody called Ma, sometimes one or two of their drivers, Julian, the kid who was going into the army and whose place I was taking, and now me.

There was a big steel staircase that led up to a balcony, and the back part of the upstairs was where the old factory had had its offices. There were two long hallways that joined a short hallway across the back in sort of a U, and all along the hallways there were steel doors with frosted glass panels in them and words painted on the glass panels to say what they had been used for. The living room was in a room marked "Production," the dining room was in "Inspection and Quality Control," the kitchen was in "Payroll and Personnel," and there were bedrooms in rooms like "Design," "Sales," "Management," "Shipping," "Receiving," and "Inventory." Across the back hall were the only rooms that were still being used for what they were put in for, as bathrooms and locker rooms—one on one side for all the men, and one on the other side for Ma.

My bedroom was in "Inventory," and there was a bed, a table, a lamp, and about a million little wooden compartments in greasy wood shelving all around the room. There was a window that I could crank open, and a drainpipe I could crawl down if it came to that.

It was a terrible place in a lot of ways. There was soot from the railroad on everything—in the water fountains, in my bed, even on the commode seats, which always gave me a bad feeling. You got to where you could even tell how much soot you were eating on sandwiches and in salads by the crunch. You got to where you didn't even mind it after a while.

And I have to admit that I liked it—not the soot, but the factory. It was the first time I ever slept in a room by myself, without 20 or 30 other kids around, and there were other things I liked, like getting and having my own radio by my bed and listening to it as late as I wanted.

I didn't like all those storage compartment boxes too much because there were families of mice that lived in them, and every once in a while there would be a rat. The Rhoduses kept cats, lots and lots of cats, and they liked hunting around in my room, which I didn't mind. I kept traps set everywhere, but the cats seemed to know where they were and what they were for and never got caught in them.

I say I liked it there; it has just now occurred to me that while I was there it was summer, and the thick brick walls kept everything dark and cool. I don't know what it would have been like in the winter, and I don't remember seeing any heaters around. I know the big old bathrooms would have been cold.

Anyway, that's where they put me to sleep. I came in and put my stuff on the bed and straightened it all out. Then I was starving and went back to "Payroll," where everybody was, to eat.

That will have to wait because it's lights out again here in a few minutes. Mr. Jackson, the night jailer, is nice to me because he knows you real well, and he knows what I'm trying to do.

The Rhoduses' agreement to feed me.

The food here in the jail is pretty bad. Every morning
this week, for instance, breakfast has been oatmeal, pow-
dered milk, an apple, and an Oreo cookie. The other pris-
oners eat it like it comes, but I've discovered a trick. I take
the filling out of the cookie, because it's sugar, and sweeten
the oatmeal, then I put the chocolate cookie parts in the
milk and thicken it up. It's hard to eat the apple right now
because I have loose teeth left over from getting busted in
the mouth. I could cut it into slices and eat it with a knife if
they would give me a knife, but they won't.

The dinners here are worse—things like cold tuna fish
on cold toast—and the suppers are just plain terrible. Last
night it was two slices of bologna that were burned, curled,
and greasy from having been cooked in a skillet.

Which is exactly how Ma Rhodus used to cook it, only
she did it worse. She'd cook it in the afternoon because she
was hungry, then she'd leave it out in the skillet all day and
warm it up for the rest of us. The only thing I can say good
about bologna is that after it gets ripe like that, catfish really
love it. You can cut it into strips and it looks to them like
worms and smells like dead feet.

Which is what I'm trying to say about Ma's cooking,
that it was and still is 10 times worse than here at the jail. I
had all night to try to think of some way to tell you how bad
it was, and that's what I came up with.

21

But, luckily, she didn't expect anybody to eat it, and nobody did. Ma hated to cook and only did it because she was a ma and her conscience hurt her if she didn't give it a try. The first night I was there, supper was a big can of beans in the skillet and whatever you could find to go with them. She'd put out some things on the table for suggestions, a package of weenies, some of her fried bologna, an onion, some leftover rice, and some leftover butter beans, like she really expected people to mix beans and beans.

And that was the way most of the meals went. Ma would put stuff out on the table and if you were hungry you ate it. She did for people exactly the same thing she did for the cats: she put it out, and if they were hungry they ate it. If they didn't like what she had, they could go find something on their own.

Which is exactly what I did. I took the bologna and crossed the tracks to the Yazoo Canal, where there were always black people fishing and extra poles and a fire going and somebody cooking fish, and I ate pretty good, unless it was raining and the banks were slick and it was too dangerous to be over there.

Roy and Thurman drank more beer than they ate food, and ate most of the time in honky-tonk cafés. I don't know what Julian did because he was gone two days after I got there. He was an orphan, like me, but unlike me his parents were still alive; they'd just abandoned him, which made him pretty tough. He was somebody who was going to have fun in the army. He already had a mustache, a little thin one, but black like Boston Blackie's, and sinister-looking.

Ma ate everything. She was about five-and-a-half feet tall and weighed a ton. Her head was as round as a human head could get, and she had thin, white, curly hair that fit exactly round around it. When I first saw her, the light was coming from in back of her head and it made her look like a dandelion ball, like you could blow on her real hard and she'd go bald.

She was always eating, usually out of a bowl. She'd eat ice cream in a bowl that she'd carry with her as she walked around; you could hear her spoon clinking against the glass, trying to get every last melted bit, and the cats would be following her everywhere she went, waiting for her to finish and put the bowl down for them, which she always did.

All over the upstairs part and the downstairs part of the building there were empty bowls. Once a day she'd ask me to go pick them up, or if I weren't around, she'd get them all herself.

What Ma did was talk on the telephone to her bingo buddies, listen to the radio shows and soap operas, talk some more on the telephone to her bingo buddies, put out something for supper, take a shower, then go play bingo till midnight with her bingo buddies. That was what she did, and all she did, except for shopping once a week and going now and then to the picture show.

I did my own cooking, washed my own clothes, ironed them if I needed them ironed, made my own bed, and did whatever else I needed to do. I have no complaints about any of this I'm telling you right now, your honor; I just wanted you to know what the Rhoduses, as their part of the agreement, did for me. For giving me a place to sleep, such as it was, and feeding me, such as as they did, the state gave them $30 a week.

Now look at what I did for them.

My day started at five in the morning, five in the morning every morning, Saturdays, Sundays, rain or shine, sick or well. It started with Roy, who was always the one coming into my room and picking my foot up by my right big toe

23

and shaking it till I woke up. Sometimes, though, he'd make it hurt with his sharp thumbnail.

"Get up, Bub," is what he'd always say. He never called me anything but "Bub."

The first thing I had to do was fill the big coffee pot downstairs and start it perking so there'd be coffee when everybody came to work. The next thing I had to do was check all the vehicles for low tires, oil, and water in the radiator and the battery, look for anything leaking out of hoses, then clean all the windshields.

The Rhodus Brothers' fleet of trucks included the old pickup without the floorboard, a medium-sized moving van, and a water truck that they used to deliver water to people out on farms whose wells had gone dry, and to road crews where they needed to spray water to keep the dust down. There was also a wrecker, or tow truck, which I'll tell you more about later, a bus that was under contract to a baseball team, and a long black limousine that looked like a big snapping beetle, which they used to deliver dead bodies to funeral homes in other towns.

That's what, six vehicles that I checked every morning.

Coffee, vehicles, then I got to go to the bathroom and wash up and find something to eat, but I didn't have forever to do it in. A driver named Eddie, who was married and lived with his wife somewhere in town, got there at six and got some coffee, and then we took off in the pickup for the train station, where we loaded up with 14 bundles of Memphis *Commercial Appeal* newspapers. Since there were 50 papers in every bundle, we had a paper route that was 700 papers.

That was my third job of the day. Between six and eight in the morning I rode in the back of that truck, rain or shine, sick or well, and delivered papers.

Only I didn't ride in the back, exactly. I straddled the rail behind the right side of the cab. I wore an old army fatigue jacket with the arms cut out, mainly because it had big pockets. I kept rubber bands in the left pocket and in my mouth, and in the right pocket I kept the wire cutters for cutting the bundles. I held on with the inside of my legs, kept my right leg on the running board to keep from being thrown out, and kept my left knee on the cut bundles while I was rolling them, which kept them from getting blown out. I had to roll and throw about 400 papers to houses; I put out about 100 in apartment buildings, and the rest went to newsstands, hotels, and downtown stores.

That gets us up to eight in the morning.

At eight I came back and worked with another crew, most of the time at first with the van crew, which worked on contract for grocery stores and furniture stores and factories like the garment factory.

I hated the van work because it was hard, dangerous, and nobody was ever happy. The Rhodus brothers weren't happy because they never contracted for enough money to make much of a profit, and the jobs always turned out to be too hard. Marcus Furniture, say, would hire us to pick up some crates at the freight depot and deliver them somewhere, and the crates would turn out to be pianos and the place they would want them delivered would be upstairs. The people we worked for were never happy, either, because they would be afraid we were going to drop something, or scratch something, or bruise something. Which sometimes we did.

Your honor, once I had to help deliver a dozen cases of some kind of rare brandy that Napoleon was supposed to have liked to drink, and the guy in charge, a guy named Sammy, stole three bottles out of one of the cases and made me drop it all down a flight of concrete steps to a basement under a hotel, figuring that everything would get broken so bad that nobody'd figure out the stealing, and since I was only 14 years old, nobody'd get too mad at me. But you should've heard the cussing I got, and Roy slapped the side of my head so hard my ears were ringing for two days.

I didn't even get any of the brandy, which was OK because I didn't drink at the time and still don't, except on special occasions. I would like to have tasted it, though, to see what Napoleon liked.

That was the morning, and for a while the afternoons were pretty much the same. I worked with the van crew, picking up things from one place, putting them down on the truck and taking them somewhere, picking them up off the truck and putting them down somewhere else. I did so much picking up and putting down that I was doing it in my sleep and waking up tired.

And now my writing fingers are tired. I've worn a blister on the finger that holds the pencils, and all the points need sharpening and they still won't let me have a knife. I'll try to see if I can get Mr. Jackson to sharpen them for me when he comes to work this evening.

Thursday, October 14, 1948

Dear Judge, your honor,

I feel like I'm starting out anew because Mr. Harmon, my lawyer, came to see me this morning and read what I wrote and said it was fine, and took it all with him for his secretary to type up. He said to start dating my letters to help him keep them straight, just keep going like I was going, and talk to you just like you were here in the cell with me. Then he told me he was trying to get me out of jail, but couldn't do much because you were out of town on vacation, and that makes it hard. How can I pretend that you're in the room with me when you ain't even in town, I want to know?

Mr. Harmon also gave me a list of the next three things that I should explain. He said I should say how I got started in gambling, and how I got tangled up with Jimmy D. Watley, and how it was that I became a fugitive from the law, which, till my trial, I didn't even know I was.

OK, the gambling.

I can say, truthfully, that I never intended to be a gambler of any kind or in any fashion whatsoever. I don't even particularly like gambling, because it seems to me that all it is is somebody who is better or smarter at something taking advantage of somebody who is worse.

27

But I did it, and I kept doing it, and I kept winning more and more money, and eventually it almost got me killed.

The way it got started was through Ma. You will remember that I told you she played bingo, and she did. She did more than play: She lived for it.

On Monday and Friday nights there were big bingo games at the Elks Club on Madison Street. On Tuesday nights the game was at the VFW, on Wednesday nights at the Moose, and on Thursday nights you had your choice of games: at the Knights of Columbus or at the Knights of Labor Temple. On Saturday afternoons there was penny bingo at the VFW Ladies' Auxiliary, and at five o'clock all the women quit, got up, went home and fixed supper, and then headed for the American Legion hut for a night game. There wasn't a regular game on Sundays, but sometimes churches would put on a game for charity.

It was always supposed to be for charity, and that was supposed to make it legitimate and something other than gambling. The Elks had bingo to support their crippled children's fund, the Moose to support the Christmas parade, and so on. . . .

The first week I was with the Rhoduses, Ma took me to bingo. It was a Monday night and the game was at the Elks, and it was not like what I had imagined.

First of all, there was a lot of pushing and shoving and squabbling over cards and who was going to sit where. Your honor, I can't even begin to tell you about the importance of bingo cards to those women. Some cards were lucky and some were cursed, some were marked up with good luck stars and some had hex marks all over them. There were cards with women's names just signed right across the top, and sometimes those cards got taken by other people, or stolen, or the names got crossed out, and real fights would

28

sometimes start. When you win the big jackpot with a card, you tend to think of it as your card.

And the same women play the same cards year after year after year. "I'm going to play old Mrs. Jamison's card tonight since she's not here. . . ." You hear things like that all the time.

Because in bingo all you've got is your cards. You can't tell them what numbers to call, you've just got to have the numbers in all the right places. B-3 and 12 in the corners. I-19 and 30 at the top and bottom for the Frame game. G-54 and 56 for the x. And so on.

Anyway, it was my first week with Ma and my first game and she thought I might be lucky, so she sent me to pick out the cards. "Pick 20," she said, "and pick ones with nothing on them." She gave me that warning and waited for me at one of the tables. There were six long tables at the Elks, three on each side of the room, and each table sat about 50 women. So there you've got about 300 women playing an average of 10 cards apiece, say 3,000 cards at a nickel a card. That meant the Elks Club was taking in, say $150 a game.

Ma would pay for her cards one game at a time, a dollar even for 20 cards, and then on the fifth game that night she bingo'd and we counted the pot, and it was $40.

And I didn't say anything, but it seemed to me like that crippled children's fund was making a whole lot of money. Ma didn't care who was making what, though, as long as she was winning. She won two more games before the intermission, and then came what is known as the "Dollar Roll."

There are three periods at the Elks Club, each one lasting about an hour. The first period, which we'd just played, was nickel bingo. Then after intermission, so the women could all go to the bathroom, it was the "Dollar Roll," which cost a dollar a card—not for each game, but for the next 10 games in a row, which were all fancy games like the +, the x, the Frame, the Four Corners, the T, the H, the S, and the U. Then came the Jackpot, which is cover the card in 52 numbers or less for $500. If nobody hits in 52 numbers for $500, they add $50 to the regular pot and it goes to 53 numbers for the next time they play, and so on till somebody hits it.

The night I first played, the Jackpot was up to 60 numbers, the highest it had ever been, and $900. Every woman in the place was playing as many cards as she could watch, and there wasn't room for another one on any table anywhere.

Ma had hit three of the nickel games for over $100, and the X game for $350, and then I'll be durned if she didn't have to wait for the jackpot on the fiftieth number. I-30 she was waiting for, and everybody around her knew it because she started telling them about it.

"I got a wait! I got a wait!" she started saying, and it was sort of like she was praying, and sort of like she was moaning and in pain. I'd say it started out more like praying. "Come on, I-30 . . . Come on, I-30," it started, and then the caller, a man named Ward, called out "Under the O—" and she moaned and just about died, dreading what he was going to say next because it meant somebody else might win.

"Seventy," he called, and nobody said anything, and Ma swelled up again like a walrus, closed her eyes, and started praying, "I-30 . . . I-30 . . . Come on, I-30 . . ."

And the caller said, "Under the I—" and Ma sucked in her breath, closed her eyes, and clenched her teeth, and he said, "29," and it was just like you had a blowout on the highway.

And then it got up to the fifty-seventh number, and she had four waits, and everybody around her had waits, and she didn't think it was fair because she'd been waiting for

I-30 forever. And by that time she was making so much noise that she was bothering everybody in the place. The caller, Ward, knew what she was sitting on and liked teasing her. On the next number out of the tumbler he looked right at her and smiled and said, "Under the I—" and he made her wait till she opened her eyes to see what was wrong, and then he said "30," and the place almost went wild. Everybody started cussing and beating on the tables and, if there hadn't been laws against it, would have gladly killed her.

She had won more money that night, that first night I went with her and picked out the cards, than any player had won at any game of bingo in the history of Vicksburg, almost $1,400.

The third period of the night at the Elks, after another intermission, was nickel bingo again, and we didn't hang around for that. We took the money and got out during the intermission, with women all around us wanting to know who I was and some of them wanting to rub my head.

That was my introduction to gambling, and because of it Ma wanted me to go play bingo with her from then on, and pick out the cards. Luckily, nobody can keep up that kind of luck very long, and pretty soon I was picking cards that turned out to be terrible and she was losing money again like a normal person.

But that first night is still important, because some of the thrill of her winning rubbed off. I hate to admit it, but every time they called a number that wasn't hers, I was dying, too. And when she won, I couldn't help it, I jumped up out of my chair and went jumping all the way down the aisle, and they had to grab me and hold me down, it was that exciting.

And there's more about winning I could say. It doesn't matter whether it's in bingo or in pool or in poker, winning gets your juices going and all your nerves on edge so that when it's all over and you've won, you're starving. Winning has never failed to make me hungry enough to eat a horse.

That's why, I've noticed, there always seems to be some kind of restaurant or food for sale around where people gamble. Around racetracks, for instance, there's always tons of steak houses.

In front of the Elks Club that first night, just like he was waiting there for us, there was a man with a cart full of hot tamales, and Ma was starving too and bought him out. We went home that night like we'd gone to battle and won the war, with $1,400 in cash and nine dozen hot tamales.

Which I had to learn to eat, as they were not like anything I'd ever eaten before. They were each one about the size of my hand, a little bit bigger than a big minnow, and they came wrapped in corn shucks. You got them out of the shuck and you leaned your head back a little, and held them up, and let them sort of slide down your throat while you kind of pressed them apart with the back of your tongue.

I tell you all of this, your honor, because it's the only way I know to tell you what gambling, at least at first, was like. Nothing has ever tasted so good in my life as those tamales did that first night.

And that's how I got started gambling.

How I got started with Jimmy D. Watley is another story, which I will tell you about in my letter tonight.

Thursday night, October 14, 1948

How I got hooked up with Jimmy D. Watley.

It all started in August when the guy who drove the tow truck, a man named Louis Duke, got beat up real bad and had to quit.

The reason he got beat up so bad was because people hated him. The Rhodus brothers had a contract with the city and with the downtown merchants' bunch to haul away cars that were parked in no-parking and unloading zones, and nothing you can do to people makes them quite as mad as hauling away their cars. They go absolutely and completely crazy, and if you're the one who's doing the hauling, you had better be on your toes, which Louis Duke wasn't. Some men caught him trying to haul away their truck, which was blocking an alley that just happened to be closed on the other end, too, and there wasn't anywhere for Louis to go. They beat him with boards and brickbats and put him in the hospital.

So the Rhoduses decided to change their tactics and hire somebody who people were afraid of, and they hired Jimmy D. Watley, and put me to working with him. They wanted me working with him for two reasons: first, I was a kid and they figured nobody would want to hurt or kill a kid; and second, I was agile enough to get under the cars and get the chain hooked around the axle real fast and get faster you got away with a car you were hauling, better, because when you were down underneath a car like that you were at a disadvantage.

With me hooking up the chain, Jimmy D. could keep a lookout, and we wouldn't get caught by surprise like Louis Duke did. That all made sense, and I was glad to get off the van crew. Hooking up chains to cars was a lot easier than hauling pianos up stairs.

And Jimmy D. was just as tough as people said he was; you could look at him and see that. He wore fancy jet-black cowboy shirts and pants. Black all over, that was his style and all he ever wore, except for his boots, which were kind of off-white—"bone white" I guess you could call them, the color of bad teeth—and except for his belt, which was made out of the same color leather as the boots, so as to match. Across the back of the belt, with roses all around it that were dyed red, he had his first name and his middle initial, "Jimmy D."

He was about six feet tall, I'd say, and shoulder-strong, like a cowboy or like somebody who'd been doing prison work, and he scared me to death. I worked with him a week before I even dared to look at him straight in the eye, and there was no way I'd ever dare to say anything.

He was about 30, and deaf in his right ear from sleeping too close to the artillery in the war, which he told me once he loved, and he had a sharp, pinched face that was crooked on one side. His face was covered with holes and the look in his eyes when he looked at people was like he was tired of seeing human beings as a whole, and them in particular.

I figured a man would have to be a complete fool to fight with Jimmy D., and if you could have seen him, your honor, you would have seen what I meant.

It was also a well-known fact that Jimmy D. carried a gun. It wasn't against the law for him to have it, because he had some kind of license. The way it was explained to me, he could carry it for as long as he was working as a bodyguard or private detective and some employer was willing to sign a legal document that they were paying him to work, which the Rhoduses did.

Officially, Jimmy D. was in charge of security for the Rhodus Brothers' Hauling and Delivery. Unofficially, he drove the tow truck, if that explains things. He also did other jobs for people in town; it was also well known, for instance, that if somebody owed you a lot of money, for a percentage you could send Jimmy D. to collect it, and sometimes all you had to do was *say* you were sending Jimmy D. to collect it and the person paid up. If Jimmy D. heard about you doing that, though, he'd get mad. His reputation was what earned him his living, and he was proud of it and protected it, and in a way I don't blame him.

Anyway, by that time it was August, and it was as hot as anybody could remember it ever being, and after I finished with the paper route, I went over and started with Jimmy D. and the tow truck.

And here's the best part: we rearranged the paper route so that we'd finish downtown, and Eddie would drop me off in front of the pool hall, where Jimmy D. would have the tow truck parked around the corner, and where he would be inside waiting.

And Judge Francis, your honor, I have to tell you about the pool hall, because for me it was like starting a whole second life.

First of all it was called Hoot's, and it was right in the middle of downtown Vicksburg on the corner of Washington and Clay, which is kind of a famous corner from the old riverboat days. You can stand outside Hoot's and roll a car tire down the hill and it won't stop till it goes in the Yazoo Canal, that is really part of the Mississippi River. Hoot's has a kind of overhanging canopy thing over the sidewalk, which makes the front of it real dark, and under the canopy there's a shoeshine stand, and piles of newspapers from big cities all around that have anything to do with cotton: Chicago, St. Louis, Jackson, Natchez, Baton Rouge, New Orleans, and, of course, Memphis. I put out the Memphis papers myself, as they are the last on the route.

When you walk in the door, on your left there's a long café counter where they've got three big stainless-steel coffee makers that are always polished and shining, and coffee mugs that are piled halfway up the wall. There's three separate grills and three cooks working them, cooking eggs, cooking hamburgers, cooking up onions, which I love the smell of, cooking up whatever you want. You can bring fish in fresh and they'll clean them and cook them up too if you want. I love to eat, your honor, and I love the smell of places like Hoot's.

On the right as you walk in, there's the gambling counter where you can't sit down, where you've got to stand because there's no stools. They have Jackpot Charley punchboards, and Gridpicks, and special pads of paper where you can write down the name of any sports team playing or any horse running in any race anywhere in the country, put down the amount you want to bet, sign it, and give it to a man called "Big Nate," and you've got yourself a bet. Behind the counter there is this huge blackboard that reaches all the way up to the ceiling, and on the blackboard there's places to print in the names of every kind of team and game that you can think of that's in season. That August, for instance, it was baseball season, and so they had all the games being played that day from the major leagues down to the southeastern league, which as you know has teams like Vicksburg, Jackson, Pensacola, Gadsden, Shreveport, Pine Bluff, and I forget who else. It was the Vicksburg team, the Billies, that rented the Rhodus Brothers' bus.

There was a ticker tape machine right there behind the

counter, and the pool hall had a kid a lot littler than me who would check the tape every time it would start ticking, then climb up a ladder and get on a catwalk that stretched across the front of the blackboard, and chalk in new scores. You could bet on such things as who would win, what the score would be, and what inning the teams would get the most runs.

There were people who came to the pool hall early in the morning, ate breakfast and read the papers there, started watching the board and gambling, ate dinner, gambled some more, ate supper there, and kept on gambling till the place closed at night. Then next morning they'd be back, doing the same thing: talking sports, talking baseball, talking about the Yankees, or the Dodgers and Jackie Robinson, who was the new second baseman and was black, and talking about St. Louis, which was Vicksburg's closest big-league team. Sports was their whole life.

If you kept walking down the building (and this was the way just about all good pool halls were), you'd pass the drinking bar, and then you got to the back part where they had the booths for women, the tables for dominoes, and the pool tables.

Now back to Jimmy D. I didn't know what he looked like or even what his name was at first because Louis Duke had just quit. Eddie dropped me off in front of Hoot's and told me, "Just walk on in and look for a man named Jimmy D. You'll see his name on the back of his belt, and he'll be waiting for you."

Which I did, smelling those onions and all the cigar and cigarette smoke, looking around at everybody's butt, and scared right down to the bottom of my feet.

I had hoped to find him up front, but that wasn't my luck. Nobody in front had Jimmy D. on his belt and I had to go all the way to the back. The back wasn't crowded because it was still morning, but there were people back there and I could hear the crack of a rack of pool balls getting busted. Then I heard somebody yell a cussword real loud and somebody else start laughing. It was Jimmy D. and another man who were shooting 9-ball, a game where whoever makes the 9-ball wins, and Jimmy D. had just made the 9-ball on the break.

When Jimmy D. wasn't being a bodyguard or collecting bad debts from people, he was hustling pool, your honor, and right from the start I kind of looked on him as a hero. I think anybody would've.

My fingers are getting sore and that's just the start of it. It's a lot easier to talk, I've discovered, than write.

Friday, October 15, 1948

Jimmy D. (continued) and how we got to be partners.

I can still remember exactly the first words Jimmy D. ever said to me, and I'm not talking about things like "Get in" and "Get out" and "Hurry up" or "Let's go," I'm talking about friendly words. We were in Hoot's and we were sitting on stools at the liquor bar right in the middle of the building, which was Jimmy D.'s favorite place because he could see everything that went on, up front, in the back, and on both sides of the room because of the mirrors.

"How many guns do you think are in here right now?" Those were his first friendly words.

My words back were something like, "I don't know . . . none?" I hadn't really been paying attention to that kind of thing.

"You better start using your eyes, kid," he said, "else you better keep your ass out of pool halls."

And that's the way he left it, just like that. Which made me start using my eyes, because I liked being in Hoot's. I looked everybody over once, twice, looking for guns, but I'll be durned, your honor, if I saw any.

"There's three," he said, and he told me where to look.

"That guy sitting at the café counter—white shirt, bald head, and khaki pants. . . ." I saw who he meant. "That's Deputy Dog. He's a sheriff's deputy out in the county and he keeps a pearl-handled, snub-nosed .38 down in his right boot." I watched, and every once in a while Deputy Dog's right pants leg came up and there it was.

"That guy shooting pool on the second table—blue jeans, Hawaiian shirt, shirttail out. . . . Watch in the middle of his back when he leans over to shoot." The man leaned over and shot, and there it was, small and low in his pants. "His name is Bo-Bo and he drives a cab. He's messing around with somebody's wife right now, and he's afraid the husband's gonna kill him," he said. "Now where's the third?"

He gave me five minutes to look around again while he just sipped coffee, read the paper, and smoked cigarettes. Then he got disgusted with me and said, "There's mine," and went back to reading his paper.

And that's the way Jimmy D. thought about things, a little like he had a chip on his shoulder and a little like he didn't want anybody taking advantage of him if he could help it. It was like he took the Boy Scout motto seriously. "Be Prepared," it said, and he was.

The big thing for me was that he had started teaching me things. I think he liked me and thought I was too goofy-looking to live if I didn't learn how to take care of myself. Maybe it was because he knew I was an orphan. Anyway, he started telling and showing me things, and one of the first things was pool.

"Always play for money. That way it means something."

He taught me the rules to straight pool and we played to 50, and he beat me 50 to about three. We were playing for a half dollar and I handed it to him. A half dollar to me was one-twentieth of what I got paid a week.

"Always throw it on the table, kid, and let the winner pick it up. That way everybody gets to see what you were playing for. Let 'em see you pay. Shows you got class," he said.

I threw the 50 cents on the table and he picked it up, and smiled, and said, "Now how about another game? For a dollar?" and I said, "No," and hung my cue up. I wasn't about to be working like I was doing for nothing. I still was making plans on escaping and needed my money too much to be giving it to him.

Which tickled him to death. "That's right, kid," he said. "When you play for money, you learn fast or you quit."

Well, I had every intention of quitting, but once he'd shown me how easy it was to play pool—it had always looked hard when I watched other people playing it—I found myself thinking about it. It's hard to explain, but I kept seeing angles that you could shoot balls and make them go in . . . and I kept seeing bank shots you could make. It was all right there in my mind. It was like I could play pool just by thinking about it, sort of like I could fish and see the bobber going up and down and play the thing. I could make pool shots, I just knew I could.

But playing cost money, and losing cost money, and I had to keep my money.

Then I made a discovery. At the Elks', and at the K of C, K of L, Moose, at the VFW and at the Legion, there were pool tables, just sitting there covered most of the time, waiting for somebody to play on them.

So I asked Ma to ask the men who ran the clubs if it would be all right if I used the tables, and they all said it was. As long as she was there playing bingo and there weren't any club members around who wanted to play, and as long as I didn't hurt anything, I was welcome. And that's how I learned to shoot; Ma played bingo three or four hours a night, and I practiced pool.

A man at the Moose showed me how to practice and get the most good out of it. You broke the rack and made as many balls as you could in a row without missing, and that was like the first inning of a baseball game. If you made six balls, you put down six; if only three, you put down three. You put them down like were keeping a box score. Then you reracked and broke again and played the bottom of the inning and so on, playing against yourself till you got to the bottom of the ninth inning and the game was over. The better your imagination, the better the games, and the better you practiced.

And the secret was to practice. I was practicing at least 20 hours a week for two weeks before I tried shooting pool again, and Jimmy D. didn't know anything about me doing it. Then it was about two weeks after he'd first shown me how, and I took a dollar out of my wallet and showed it to him, and said, "I've been saving this to shoot you another game," and he smiled and we got cues.

I beat him the first game, and he couldn't believe it, and threw the dollar down on the table like he'd shown me. "Shoot again?" I said, and he said, "Hell, yes," and I beat him the second time. Then I told him about practicing on the tables at bingo with Ma.

People in the pool hall have a way of watching what is going on, and they'd watched me beat Jimmy D. There had been a good morning crowd for the second game, so many in fact that Jimmy D. decided to quit for a while, and I was just as glad.

"Let's go haul away some cars," he said, and so we went back to work.

We didn't really have to go looking for work. Jimmy D. and Roy had set it up so that when a call came in to the garage for the tow truck to haul a car, Roy simply called us there at Hoot's. It saved time, really, because all of the illegal parking was right there downtown. It was a Friday, I remember, and my beating Jimmy D. out of a dollar had put him in a bad mood; I'll bet you we hauled away 15 cars that morning.

It was late afternoon before Jimmy D. had got over being mad and started talking to me again. By that time he'd thought of something.

Now the best pool shot in town, or anywhere around for that matter, was Bo-Bo, the man who carried the gun in the back of his pants and drove the cab. His shift was night and mornings, so he was done for the day and would be in the pool hall relaxing.

"You've seen Bo-Bo shoot?"

"I have," I said.

"Can you take him?"

"I think so," I said.

That was good enough for a start, Jimmy D. decided, so we quit and headed for Hoot's. When we got there, Jimmy D. went over and arranged a game, giving Bo-Bo some story about me getting too big for my britches and needing to be boosted out of about $20. Bo-Bo was glad to be of service, so that's what we shot for, $20, and that's what I won. Then Jimmy D. came over and whispered, "Give him that stupid look you give people," and I knew he meant my Dumas look. So I did, and Bo-Bo wanted to shoot again, for $20 more, and I beat him again, by a terrible score. Everything I shot seemed to want to go in, and everything he shot just hung there in the pockets. And that was it; he threw the money on the table and quit.

I had beat the best player in Vicksburg, and people had seen me do it, and people kind of knew who I was after that.

What I mean, your honor, is that nobody else would

play me for money. I liked to shoot, and since I had found out that I was good at it, I even *loved* to shoot, and I kept getting better at it, and better. Jimmy D. couldn't beat me anymore, couldn't even come close, and neither could anybody else. Jimmy D. sort of became my manager then, and wouldn't let me play for free. People had to put up at least a dollar to shoot against me, and after a while nobody wanted to do that.

So there we were, me going to waste and there was Jimmy D., thinking about it harder and harder.

Then the last week in August, Jimmy D. got fired.

It was another one of those busy Fridays, and it was raining, and we were hauling off a big Buick that was double parked and blocking traffic right in the middle of Washington Street, right in front of Penney's. Well, I was down under the thing, on my back in the wet and rain, and Jimmy D. was standing guard like he always did. Out of the hardware store across the street this guy comes charging out; it's his car we're hauling away, and he's gone crazy. Jimmy D. is watching the front of Penney's, and I'm trying to warn him to turn around because the guy who's running out has got an axe—that's what he's been in the hardware store to buy. It even has the big red price tag still wired to the handle.

Anyway, Jimmy D. sees him and turns around and pulls out his gun, and you could tell the guy recognized Jimmy D. all of a sudden, or saw the gun, but it was too late. Jimmy D. brought the pistol up to point between the guy's eyes, and the top part of the guy stopped cold dead still while his feet went on going. That's when Jimmy D. decided to squeeze off a shot, straight up in the air, except I didn't know it because my eyes were closed, and the guy didn't know it because he thought he was dead, and nobody else didn't know it because there he was laying in the street and there was Jimmy D. holding the pistol.

It is amazing some of the things that have happened to me. The guy wasn't dead, and got up and checked himself to see if he'd been shot. Instead of being happy that he wasn't hurt, he got mad as hell and started yelling for the police.

It turned out that the guy with the axe was the mayor's wife's brother, and he had been in the war and was a disabled veteran and all, and it was bad for Jimmy D. for a few days. The police tried to get him for firing a firearm in the city limits, but couldn't. In fact, nobody could get him for nothing—the guy had come at us with an axe.

But still, your honor, they put it in my trial and made it look like I'd done something wrong. Well, I hadn't.

And I didn't think Jimmy D. had either. Suppose, your honor, that he hadn't been Jimmy D. at all, but somebody else who didn't have a gun. Do you think the guy with the axe would have stopped, or would he have just kept coming and used it on us? That was the thing about Jimmy D. that you had to take into consideration.

Even back then, though, it was like we'd done something wrong. The Rhodus brothers started looking at Jimmy D. funny, watching him too close for it to be comfortable. They kept me working with him, even though deep in their hearts they thought he was a maniac, because they didn't think he'd do anything to hurt a kid.

What the brothers were trying to think of was a way to get rid of him without him getting mad about it, and I guess I don't blame them for that.

The next thing I have to tell you about is why Jimmy D. and I left town like we did, but I'm going to have to wait a while on that because Mr. Jackson has been blinking the light for me to quit. Today was a short day because they let me sleep late, and tomorrow is going to be short, too, 'cause they've got me scheduled to go see a doctor and dentist.

Mr. Harmon, my lawyer, says the county here has finally decided to do something about my teeth.

Monday, October 18, 1948

Dear Judge, your honor,

It has been three days since I last had a chance to do any writing on this. Mr. Harmon, my lawyer, has had me back to the dentist twice more, and they've got my mouth wired up and everything.

The next thing I was going to explain was how I got to be a fugitive from the State of Mississippi, which is another thing that looked so bad at my trial.

That part is true. If you didn't want to sentence me to anything, you could send me back to Vicksburg and they'd put me in the reform school down there because I'm in their power till I'm 17 and I've only this past April had my fifteenth birthday.

But to get back to where I was, me and Jimmy D. both knew something was coming, and he started talking to me, saying things like "You don't want to be a delivery boy all your life, do you?" and I did not, and "You hang around the Rhoduses long enough and you'll be just like them . . . that what you want?" and it was not.

"You're the best pool shot I've ever seen in my life," he said. "Not only that, you've got that stupid look on your face that makes people want to give you their money. I've never seen anything like it, but there it is and you've got it."

47

With my talent and his brains, he kept telling me, we could be rich. Fifty-fifty. He guaranteed me we'd make $300, $400 a week each. The money was out there in little towns and pool halls, just waiting for us to come into town and take it.

"You've seen how we've got to keep moving," he said. We were sitting in Hoot's at the time, as I remember, and he said, "Look around. You see anybody in here who'll shoot you a game for money?"

There wasn't nobody, and that was a good point.

It wasn't so much that I wanted to go be a pool hustler, your honor, but you remember how I'd been sent to live with the Rhoduses as a kind of punishment, and I told you how I'd been saving my money to run away anyway . . . well, this was my chance.

"All we need is a circuit we can get on," Jimmy D. said. A circuit was something like a fair, or a circus, something that traveled around that you could work for and so get your traveling and food and sleeping free, so everything you made gambling was yours to keep.

He started buying and looking through every paper he could get his hands on, and every once in a while he'd get the bartender to give him a bunch of dimes and quarters and he'd get on the phone. I watched him and knew what he was up to, though I didn't think he'd have any luck. And then one day he did.

He came back from the telephone with the Greenville, Mississippi, newspaper in his hand, and it was open to the page where they say what's on at the movies. At this one movie theater, the Strand, instead of a movie they were having a hypnotist show being put on by a guy named Dr. Polgart. There was a picture of him and he was one scary-looking person. Under the picture it said, "Last time tonight." It was a Friday morning paper and we were reading it on a Friday afternoon.

"If we can get there in time, we've got a job," he said, and I said, "Yes." He took me back to the garage and I slipped upstairs and packed up my stuff. Then he left in the tow truck and came back with his stuff packed and two train tickets, and I threw everything out the window of my room and he caught it in the parking lot below. We were on our way.

More tonight . . .

Monday, October 18, 1948, night

Nights in the jail are always the worst time because everybody gets lonesome. There's a guy up front named Dale who can play the harmonica, and after supper everything gets quiet and he starts playing old cowboy songs and it makes you want to cry sometimes. If I were a big record maker, I'd give him a contract and just let him play for all the people who've never been to jail and will probably never get the chance.

I've looked at the three things Mr. Harmon, my lawyer, wanted me to tell you about and I've pretty much told you about all three—how I got started gambling, how I got tangled up with Jimmy D., and how I became a fugitive.

I tried to find out what he wanted me to do next, but he's gone out of town, too, with a big new case, so Mr. Jackson tells me.

I don't know what to do next, so I'll just have to tell you about Dr. Polgart. It's not real important, so you may want to skip over it, but I'm going to tell it anyway because it all happened. It all started with the train ride to Greenville, which I liked a lot, and which is where I'll start.

In my bedroom at the Rhoduses' garage, which was on

the side of the building closest to the tracks, I used to lay in bed and listen to the trains at night and dream I was riding on them. Up to Memphis, down to New Orleans, over to Dallas or Jackson. So riding up to Greenville was something for me because the last time I was on a train I was just a baby and couldn't remember it. For Jimmy D. it must have just been an ordinary thing, though, because he pulled his boots off and stretched out on the seat across from me and went to sleep. He was smelling up the coach and the people who came through looked at us and frowned, but I didn't care.

I couldn't have slept if I'd tried. I couldn't stop looking out the window, and from a train window you can see everything. It was something to see the cotton rows growing like they were, straight as an arrow for as far as you could see and never, never a row out of line. Then there would be little towns, and you could see people looking at the train. Then the cotton would start again, and the sun started going down and everything turned purple, then gold, then it was dark and you could see the lights come on in the shacks.

There was one little place I remember that had a bayou running right through the middle of town, and on the other side of the bayou there were six big mansion houses in a row, and one of the houses was having a party. There was a barge, or a pier, all lit up with colored lanterns, and people, young people, wearing white tuxedoes like in the movies, and dancing.

I remember seeing it all and not being jealous or wishing it was all mine; I was glad enough just to be on a train and out in the world where I could see things like that and know they were real.

It's funny, but when Dale starts playing his harmonica and people start feeling homesick for someplace else, that's the place I think of, and I imagine myself at that party watching the train pass by.

We stopped for a few minutes in a town called Rolling Fork, and a family came on the train selling sandwiches and I bought one, which was my supper.

Then we got to a place called Leland, and the train started backing up. It backed all the way from Leland to Greenville, which is 15 or 20 miles, only nobody told me what was happening, and I thought we were going all the way back to Vicksburg for a while.

But we didn't. We got off in Greenville and got a cab, and Jimmy D. told the driver to take us to the Strand, and to hurry. The show was supposed to have started at 7:30 and it was getting close to 9:00.

When we got there the show was still going on, but nobody was taking up tickets anymore, so we just walked in.

We were going to sit down in the back, but it didn't turn out that way. Dr. Polgart saw us, and Jimmy D. waved to signal him that we were there and pointed at me, and I could see the doctor give him a signal back.

Then, "Go on up front and let him hypnotize you," Jimmy D. told me, and that was the first I'd ever heard of that little deal.

Jimmy D. sat in the first seat at the end of the aisle and put his foot up and wouldn't let me in and gave me a kind of push down toward the front. There were about 200 to 250 people in the place and they were all turned around in their seats looking at us, and then the doctor started waving his arm.

"Come on down front, young man," he said. "There's somebody up here who wants to meet you."

I still wasn't sure I wanted to do it, in fact I knew I didn't because I hate being up in front of people, but Jimmy D. kept saying for me to go on.

"We ain't got jobs, least you can be hypnotized," he said, and so I had to do it.

I walked down the big main aisle and people started laughing and clapping 'cause they could tell I didn't want to do it. Then, when I got down front, I stood right there in front of the stage, hoping the doctor could hypnotize me from there, but that wasn't good enough. I had to go on up. He had two guys up on stage already, both of them sitting in straight-back chairs and sound asleep—"under his power," so to speak.

When I got up on stage, he woke one of the fellows up, a guy who looked like he might be a farmer, and said, "Mr. President, there's somebody here for you to meet, somebody who's come all the way to Washington just to shake your hand." The guy got up from his chair and acted like he was straightening his tie, except he didn't have a tie, and he thought he was really Harry S. Truman, and came over and asked me how I liked being in the White House, and was I a Democrat or a Republican? What do you even say to something like that? Then after we shook hands, the doctor put the "president" back to sleep again and started working on me.

Now let me tell you how he looked. He looked a little like Count Dracula in the vampire movies; he was dressed all in dark purple and was wearing a dark purple cape and top hat. He had straight gray hair hanging down from the hat, which I later discovered was a wig, and he had a gray mustache and gray eyes which didn't quite do right. One looked right at you, and the other one never moved because it was glass. That's what hypnotized you, looking at that glass eye and listening to the doctor's soothing words. I don't know how it worked, exactly, but it did.

I think the way it worked was that I wanted for the

doctor to do good so he would hire us, so I wanted to do what he told me. "Concentrate on my eyes," he said, and I concentrated. If you've never done that, your honor, it's a little bit like being in a dark room and turning a flashlight on and shining it on something bright. You stare at the bright circle and the first thing you know it begins to shimmer and glow, and then it fades out and you kind of go blind. That's what happened to me, and the whole time the doctor was telling me that I was getting sleepy. I hadn't slept any on the train, and I was. Jimmy D. says I started snoring.

And after that, I can't say exactly what happened, but we must have put on quite a show because when I woke up and tried to walk I almost fell down. I was wearing Harry Truman's big clodhopper boots, and he was wearing my old tennis shoes. I had to check my pants and shirts to see what else I'd done, but they were all right.

People were howling with laughter and clapping, and everything me and the other guy did seemed to be funny. The doctor said "red" for example, and the guy started rolling on the floor and scratching at fleas. Then he said "blue" and the seat of my chair got as hot as a skillet on the stove. It burned the very devil out of my butt, but when I touched it with my finger, it was cold.

That was the kind of show he put on and what he wanted me to do. I was going to be the one who "volunteered" to come up out of the audience first and get hypnotized, 'cause he could do me with a snap of his fingers from that first night on. My job was that I broke the ice and showed the people in the audience that it wasn't embarrassing or dangerous to get hypnotized, and when we did the high schools, I was the one who put on the demonstration of what-all hypnosis could do, including how it could get the best of pain. I didn't know about it for a long time, but that first night in Greenville the doctor stuck a needle all the way through my little finger and told me that it wouldn't hurt, and it didn't. Then he told me that I wouldn't remember him doing it, and I didn't. Over the next three months he stuck needles through all of my fingers, my cheek, my tongue, my earlobes, the skin on my arms, the skin on my legs, then started all over again. Every time he hypnotized me he stuck a needle through something, and the next day I used to see the holes and wonder how I got them.

I didn't know any of that till Jimmy D. and him had the falling out, though. He couldn't do things like that to real volunteers, and that's why we had jobs.

So there we were in Greenville, Mississippi, joined up with a circuit. After the show, we helped the doctor pack up all his stuff, which wasn't much, in his car, and we drove out of town a little ways toward the bridge and found a café that was open and got something to eat and made our plans.

Jimmy D. was in charge of packing, unpacking, putting out the handbills and posters, and driving the car. I was the professional volunteer, and helped Jimmy D. with everything except the driving. In return for what we did for the doctor, we got to travel with him, and he'd pay for one room in the same hotel he slept in that we'd have to share, and he'd pay us two dollars a day for us to eat on, which was plenty. We had to take care of our own clothes and our own everything else. That was the deal. Our time was our own once everything else was done, and if we wanted to shoot pool with it, that was our business.

It was after midnight when we pulled out of Greenville that first night, and there wasn't any traffic on the road. We drove up onto the bridge and were crossing the Mississippi River, the first time for me, and Jimmy D. thought we ought to have some kind of celebration and stopped the car.

The doctor had a bottle of whiskey, and we all got out and took a drink out of it and gave loud howls at the moon, and Jimmy D. pulled out his pistol and squeezed off a shot. It almost scared me to death, and the poor doctor almost wet his pants.

Then we were off and running.

Tuesday, October 19, 1948

Dear Judge, your honor,

I meant to write more last night, but I got to laughing, remembering Jimmy D. and that pistol, and I got interrupted. Mr. Jackson wanted to read what I'd been writing about, and I let him. Then we got to talking and telling stories and there went the night.

He says I've been around more than any kid my age who ever lived, and I told him to wait till he reads about Sidewinder, which I am going to try to get to today.

But first I have to tell you about the circuit and my shooting pool, because that is one of the things the prosecutor kept telling the jury, that I was nothing but a no-good drifter and pool hustler who had never worked and was always out to get something for nothing.

Well, I have to admit that that's the way it started off. I didn't mind getting hypnotized, and I didn't know anything about getting the needles poked through me. And the traveling around was a lot of fun because I was seeing a lot of country and doing a lot of things; traveling like that, you can't help learning a lot about people and life.

The way the doctor's circuit went, he started in St. Louis and every weekend, Friday and Saturday nights, he put on a show in a rented movie theater in a fairly big town—Memphis, Tennessee; Greenville, Mississippi (where

57

we joined on); then Monroe and Shreveport in Louisiana; then Tyler and Wichita Falls in Texas; then up to Oklahoma City, Enid, Ponca, and Tulsa in Oklahoma. We spent a whole month in the state of Oklahoma and I was so glad to get out of there I could puke. Then we hit Joplin, Missouri, and swung back south into Arkansas, where we hit Springdale, Fort Smith, Little Rock, and finally ended up here in Hot Springs.

Fifteen weeks altogether—Louisiana and Texas in September and October, Oklahoma in October and November, (we spent Thanksgiving Day up in Fayetteville), then November and December in Arkansas.

Dr. Polgart had a two-week engagement at one of the casinos, then he was going to meet his wife and take a vacation till after the New Year, and then he was going down to do a winter tour in the sunny south.

So me and Jimmy D. would be on our own in December, he warned us. Whether we went with him down south or not would depend on how we worked out.

That was just the overall plan—the big towns, your honor, and the weekends. That doesn't mean that we just hung around and shot pool all week, though, oh no. The doctor spent weekdays and nights putting on shows in high school auditoriums in the little towns we went through on our way to the big towns. For instance, we went into Louisiana to put on weekend shows in Monroe, but we did shows in Lake Providence and Bastrop on the way. What the doctor would do would be to call ahead and talk to the high school principals and say we'd put on a free demonstration of hypnotism in general assembly if he'd let us use the auditorium that night for our regular show, which we would charge for. The principals usually said OK. (If they didn't, he'd keep on calling till he found one who did.) Then we'd set up and tell all the kids about hypnotism, and that's where I would come in. The kids would go home and tell their mamas and daddies how good the show was and how funny I was, jumping out of my seat and thinking I was the President or King Kong or somebody. Then we'd do the night show and the doctor would make some money. We wouldn't just be wasting it while we waited around for the weekends.

The way we did our traveling, which I guess I've told you, was in the doctor's old car, which was a huge Dodge with luggage racks on the top and on the trunk in back. At one time it had been an army general's car; there were holders on both bumpers, front and back, for special license plates and flags. It was khaki-colored and had a good radio; the greatest thing about it, though, was that there were three seats: the front and back seats, which were normal and faced frontwards, then there was a middle seat, which was mine, which was right behind the driver's seat and faced backwards. Sometimes when it wasn't too cold and we were in towns where the hotel was rotten, we just slept in the car, and having three seats meant my not having to sleep in the trunk. Sleeping in the car wasn't bad; the doctor had extra blankets and pillows for Jimmy D., and I had my own bedroll.

If it got real cold, I would sometimes take a sip of whiskey, which I didn't like but sipped anyway because it put circulation back in my feet. There was always whiskey around because the doctor loved it and bought it by the case. The stuff he bought was called Ole Capt'n Jack and it shouldn't ever have been put in a bottle and sold. There was a picture on the label of a one-eyed pirate who must've been Ole Capt'n Jack himself, and he had a bloody knife in one hand and a bottle of Ole Capt'n Jack in the other, like if the knife didn't kill you, the whiskey surely would. It tasted like a cross between cough syrup and gasoline, and you could probably use it for rat poison, except no rat would drink it.

Dr. Polgart liked it, though, and I had two theories on that. One: I thought maybe he liked it because Ole Capt'n Jack only had one eye. He didn't have a glass eye like the doctor did, but only a patch, but I figured it was something like "misery loves company." Two: I thought maybe the doctor *was* really a doctor and had done something terrible in his life and gotten kicked out of the profession, and he drank to punish himself, like in the movies. It might have been the only thing he could find to kill the pain. Either way, I never found out because the doctor didn't talk too much about himself except to complain about his wife, who had put together the schedule. ("She vants to kill me," he used to moan, talking with Vs instead of Ws. "She vants to kill me.")

The doctor was about 50 years old, I figured, and though he wasn't very friendly or talkative, late at night, after he'd had a few pulls on Ole Capt'n Jack, he'd loosen up and want the radio up loud and start singing along to the songs, just like the Rhodus brothers, except in German, or Polish, or some language we couldn't figure out.

When we weren't traveling, or sleeping, or eating, or helping the doctor with his shows, we were hustling pool. That was the whole purpose of our being on the trip and doing all the other stuff. And it was worth it, I guess. Every town, big ones and little ones, had a pool hall, and there was always somebody around willing to shoot.

This was our hustle:

The way we worked it, Jimmy D. and I would come in and pass out handbills and put up posters for the show, and since we just happened to be in the pool hall, we'd stop and shoot a game, usually for $5. I'd win and Jimmy D. would cuss and moan and I'd laugh and rub it in. "Twenty dollars." Jimmy D. would tell everybody, "I can't beat him, but I'd be willing to put up $20 to see somebody beat this little snot." It wasn't "snot" he called me, your honor, but Mr. Harmon told me not to cuss.

Somebody would nearly always volunteer because, since Jimmy D. was putting up the money, there wasn't any way he could lose. The secret, though, was that there wasn't any way he could win, either, because Jimmy D. had the knack of always picking out one of the worst players to go first. The guy would play me and I'd beat him, and Jimmy D. would give me the $20 and start cussing even louder, and I'd rub it in even worse.

One of the good shots would want to try me then, but Jimmy D. would show him his wallet, and he'd be out of money. I'd have $25, though, and there'd usually be somebody around who was willing to put up his own money to play me for that. Sometimes there'd be four or five who'd want to play, and that was all I ever needed, somebody with money to play against. I'd win $50 and $100 lots of times, but there were also times when we'd hit a pool hall and there wouldn't be $20 in the whole place.

In Shreveport, Louisiana, there was this guy who thought he was really hot and he could never believe I was actually beating him. He lost $200 all by himself, and two of his buddies lost another $50. That, though, was an unusual night.

So Jimmy D. and I weren't making the $400 a week apiece that he had promised, but we weren't far off. The first two weeks we made $150 apiece, and that's without any overhead, pure profit.

In Texas we even did better. I made $300 the first week and $250 the second, and I don't know how much Jimmy D. made because he was making some bets of his own on the side.

But something happened in Texas that I didn't like, and that made me feel bad. I played a guy named Ames who was a hero from the war, and I beat him. The reason I know he was a hero is that the town was a place called Queen City, and they didn't have a pool hall at all, just a couple of tables in the American Legion hut where everybody hung out. And they had this guy's picture on the wall in a place of honor with all sorts of decorations around it. He had ribbons and medals all over him like he was Audie Murphy or somebody like that, and he got treated like a hero. People kept buying him drinks, and he kept drinking them and playing me for $20 a game. He didn't have but $40 himself, but his friends kept loaning him money, and he kept making me play. He was going to keep playing me till he beat me, I figured, and so finally I let him win. Then he was going to keep playing me till he got all his money back. That was when Jimmy D. stepped in and said we had to go, and that's when we almost had to fight our way out. Hero or no hero, Jimmy D. would have killed him.

I got us out of there, your honor, by telling them all where we'd be the next night and telling them I'd play them, or anybody they wanted to bring, for any amount they wanted to play for.

And then the next night we were over in the next town, a place called Gilmer, and there they were again, six of them, all sober, and all carrying guns. I wanted to give him his money back and told Jimmy D., but Jimmy D. said that was a bad idea because it would look like charity.

The war hero had $100 even, and we shot for it, straight pool to a hundred; I beat him 100-93, and that was close enough for him not to feel bad. He paid up, and I took the money, and they went on back home.

So what I'm saying, your honor, is that I may have been a hustler because we were tricking people a little into shooting pool with me—and maybe I did start out thinking it was going to be an easy life—but that's not the way it was turning out. Taking a chance on getting killed for a measly $100 was not like getting something for nothing. And riding around the country with a crazy foreign hypnotist and getting hypnotized by him was not my idea of "not working."

What would have happened, I always wondered, if Polgart had had a heart attack and died while I was under his power? Would I have had to spend my whole life thinking I was Napoleon, or King Kong, or the president, or who even knows what? One time, Jimmy D. told me, the doctor told me I was Lassie and I was down on my hands and knees acting like a dog. What would have happened if he'd have died then?

On top of everything else, my conscience was starting to bother me, too. I was trying to take advantage of other people, no matter what Jimmy D. said.

"Don't worry about it." That's what Jimmy D. kept telling me. "The reason they shoot is because you look like easy pickings," he'd say. "All you're doing to them is what they're trying to do to you."

I knew he was right but I still couldn't help it, your honor; I felt, deep down in my heart, like what I was doing was wrong.

Tuesday night, October 19, 1948

Tonight I'm going to tell you about the circuit again, but this time telling about how our luck turned bad.

Which it did, almost the minute we got into Oklahoma, which had a law called the "Loose Stock Legal" law, which meant that cows, bulls, horses, chickens, pigs, goats, and dogs could all eat or sleep wherever they wanted to, including the middle of the highway, and if you ran over them, it would be your fault. They had it in Louisiana, too, but they didn't take advantage of it down there like the people in Oklahoma did.

Well, no sooner did we cross the Oklahoma line than we started having to dodge animals. Cows and horses, big goats and pigs were pretty much safe, but the little animals, especially the chickens, were on their own as far as Jimmy D. was concerned, and one night he had so many feathers flying you'd have thought we were a tornado.

Just outside Chickasha, which is a good name for it, the Oklahoma Highway Patrol was waiting and fined us $100. Two dollars, we figured, per chicken, when you could buy them in the stores for practically nothing.

The first luck that went bad was the doctor's. It seemed like every time we showed up at a high school, something was going on. "I'm sorry," the principal would say, "when I told you to come on I forgot about the senior play . . ." or the spaghetti supper, or the charity bingo game, or the busted water pipes, or the new coat of paint on the auditorium floor, which was where they also played basketball, or the pep rally, or the band concert . . . you name it and it was going on.

That made us start driving more and more out of our way to find work. Then on the weekends the doctor would have the movie theater rented but it would be a football night, and folks in Oklahoma liked football about as much as they liked church.

Then my and Jimmy D.'s luck started going bad. We went through a whole stretch of towns where there wasn't a spare dollar in the whole town, much less in the pool hall. Lots of places didn't have pool halls at all, and sometimes when they did you kind of wished they didn't. In a town called Perry, for example, they had a store, and the store had a pool table. But the table didn't have a rail all along the left side, so when you shot up against it, your pool balls just went "Bonk." In another place they had a rail, but it was an old tractor-tire thread that had been straightened out and nailed to the sides with two-penny nails.

The worse thing I saw was in a place that had been an old cow town, and had a beautiful pool hall and saloon—big wide wooden floors, a big old cowboy bar, deer heads and longhorn cows' heads mounted on plaques on the walls, a fancy chandelier, and a stage for dancing girls and everything. Only it wasn't a pool hall and saloon anymore; the owner and his wife had been in a car wreck and almost died, but didn't, and both of them had decided to give up their evil lives, and they'd turned it into a "salvation hall." There were pictures from the Bible everywhere, and instead of liquor they sold ice cream and malted milks and sodas. All around the walls, mixed in with the deer heads and cow heads, there were sayings from the Bible. The funniest thing, though, was across the back wall, where there was a banner that had in big letters, "John 3:16." What made it funny, your honor, and I don't mean to be poking fun at anybody's religion, was it was right over the door to the john. They didn't even know what a john was.

Of course there was no gambling in that place.

In some of the towns we went to, the whole town was full of Indians, and they didn't even know what pool was.

Then there was another kind of trouble, and that was with Jimmy D.

When we crossed over into Oklahoma, I had right at $800 saved up. And though we weren't making real big money any more, we were still making about $100 a week, more or less, depending on how we did in the big places— Oklahoma City, Enid, and Ponca. I spent some of my money on stuff I needed. I bought a used suitcase and some clothes; I also got myself a good coat because I was freezing to death, and a raincoat because I was tired of getting wet. I hardly ever spent any money on other things, though, because there wasn't anything but going to shows to spend it on.

So I know how much Jimmy D. had to start with, the same as I did, except that he had things to spend it on, your so-called "adult things," which were mainly hanging out in honky-tonks and spending it on beer and on women. When we were stuck someplace and couldn't work, I'd go to the movies and come back to the hotel, and Jimmy D. would have the door locked and wouldn't let me in. All up and down the hall you could smell the cheap perfume and hear women giggling, and I'd end up having to sleep in the car. Once, the doctor and Jimmy D. were having their little party together, and the doctor came out and hypnotized me, and the next thing I knew, it was the next day and I was back in the car riding. The doctor put me to sleep and had me crawl up under the bed.

What would have happened, your honor, if the hotel

had caught fire? I started getting mad at their doing that kind of stuff.

Finally we got shed of the state and crossed over into Missouri, and almost immediately our luck changed again. The last thing Jimmy D. did before we left Oklahoma was run over one last bunch of chickens, though he did make a small attempt not to do it.

Joplin, Missouri, your honor, is a good town with lots of money and lots of people in the sporting life. Jimmy D. told me back in the old days it was where all the traveling salesmen crossed paths, and so it was always lively with lots of drinking and gambling, and it's still going on today. He promised me we'd do well 'cause I was a veteran now, and we did. I'll have to tell you about all that tomorrow because I've just gotten a present from Mr. Jackson. He brought me a harmonica because I said I liked them, and Dale is going to show me how to play, which won't be easy because I still have my teeth wired up.

Wednesday, October 20, 1948

The next thing I have to tell you about is Joplin, be-cause that's where things turned back the other way.

The pool hall in Joplin was called The Lucky Seven, and you couldn't see from one end of the place to the other because of the smoke. Of all the places we hit on the circuit, this one was the most like Hoot's. Mainly, it was full of peo-ple who had money to spend and weren't afraid of spend-ing it. There were nine pool tables and four domino tables all going at the same time sometimes, and every time a game would end, you could see the money changing hands—$10 bills, $20 bills. The people up there liked to gamble, just like the people in Hot Springs do.

So we passed out the handbills and asked the owner if it'd be all right to put up a poster, and we were putting it up when a guy came up to us and he looked familiar, and he said, "Louisiana." I didn't know what he meant, then he said, "Shreveport," and I knew. He'd been in the pool hall in Shreveport the night I'd won $250 and he remembered me. He was, of all things, a pool hall supplies salesman, and he had a favor to ask.

"My brother-in-law owns the company," he said, "and thinks he's a hotshot pool player." He wanted to fix it up for me to take his brother-in-law for some money, and he told us, "He hates to lose more than anything in the world. Just beat him once and he'll go crazy."

He went to the phone to call his brother-in-law, whose name, he said, was Cracker Johnson. Jimmy D. and I went back to our hotel to get more money. Actually, we went to get my money because Jimmy D. was down to about $100.

"What I figure is this," Jimmy D. said. "The guy ain't his brother-in-law at all, but some hustler he knows. So what he'd do is lose the first game and put on an act and want to play for more, and if a pool salesman is willing to back him, you got to figure he'll be good. We haven't seen him shoot and he hasn't seen us, so I say we make the first game expensive and make him play."

"What happens if I lose?" I asked him. It was my money that was being put up, and if I lost I was going to be out two months of hard work.

"You've got to learn not to love money," he said. "The only thing money's good for is to spend or use as chips. Mine's been spent, so yours is the chips."

And he was right, your honor. If you're going to be a gambler, you can't love money. So I got my money and back to the pool hall we went.

And a funny thing had happened. There wasn't hardly anybody shooting. The owner of the place had the vacuum cleaner out and was cleaning his best table, and a crew was in there with a level making sure that it wasn't falling off to either side, and when we got there, there was the guy from Shreveport with a whole bunch of fancy new cues, the kind that you carried around in a little satchel and screwed together when you wanted to play. What weight cue did I like, he asked me, and I told him 20. What kind of tip did I like, and I said half-inch, and he handed me one and said he'd be proud if I shot with it. It was a $100 cue, and if I took money off Cracker Johnson, it would be mine to keep. All he wanted was a picture of me holding it and smiling.

Then I tried it out and it was like pointing a magic

wand. The table was perfect, the cue was perfect, and since I didn't have anything to hide anymore, I wasn't bad myself.

Then Cracker Johnson came in, and we shook hands, and he and me and Jimmy D. and the guy from Shreveport, whose name was Bill Manning, all got together and talked.

"How about a game for a $100?" Cracker offered us, and Jimmy D. looked at me and winked. "No," Jimmy D. told him back, "we don't need to hustle each other, not with all these people watching. I'd be ashamed to waste their time like that." "Five hundred dollars?" Cracker said, and Jimmy D. said, "One thousand dollars." All of a sudden, you could tell, Cracker wasn't so sure of himself.

He was, I'd say, in his 40s, and looked like a cultured man. I mean by that he wasn't a bum. He looked like he wore suits all the time, not just for special occasions like the Rhoduses, and his shoes were old but shined. He had been to the barber shop recently, and smelled like Rose Hair Tonic. The only thing strange about him was his left ear—there was a half-moon plug missing out of the rim like some tiny little kid had taken a bite out of it. He saw me looking at it and said, "Bullet hole."

Anyway, your honor, we shot. For that kind of money we decided to play straight pool to 125. He took the first big lead 31-9, and then I caught up. We shot even for the next two racks and were about tied 69-68. Then I took the lead when he left a ball sitting perfect for a run, and I ran the next two racks and had him down 96 to 70. He made a short run back, but I started playing hard defense and made him take bigger and bigger chances. I had him 120-102, and he left me hard against another ball and it looked like I had no possible shot, but I saw one he didn't think I knew about. It's a way of shooting through the ball you're frozen against and making another ball, which I said I was going to try to do, and did. He didn't even wait for me to finish shooting. He didn't go crazy, he just put his money on the table and quit, and Bill Manning got to take his picture. I don't know if Cracker Johnson was his brother-in-law or not, and I didn't care. All I knew was that I'd played my first big-time pool game against a player who knew what he was doing, and I'd won—$1,000 and a brand-new cue.

Jimmy D. got $500 and was happy to have money again, and to prove he meant what he said when he said money was to spend, he did something I didn't expect and will always have to remember him for doing. When we got back to the hotel that night, we weren't in the same room anymore. He had got me my own room, and when I went up to go to bed there was somebody there waiting for me, and she said she was going to be my teacher. She had one of those beauty spots on her cheek and said her name was Desiree, and said that she was French, and she had a bottle of French champagne to prove it.

When Mr. Harmon, my lawyer, reads all that, he'll probably make me take it out. Sometimes, though, you just like to remember the good times you've had and brag a little. Especially when you're sitting in jail.

Thursday, October 21, 1948

It's night again. And raining. I don't have a window where I can see it, but I can hear it on the roof and I can smell it. Mr. Jackson just came in from the outside with his feet all wet.

I was telling you about the circuit; now I'll go through how it ended, because there were a couple of things that happened that were important.

Thanksgiving we spent in Fayetteville. We were in a hotel right across the street from the pool hall and right down the street a block from the movie theater that the doctor had rented. It was the most convenient situation we'd ever been in, but it didn't do any of us any good. The college and schools were all closed for the holiday, so the doctor had to take a holiday, too. The old pool hall was open, except it wasn't open for business, exactly. Everything was free because it was Thanksgiving, and they were having a big Thanksgiving dinner.

They had moved all the domino tables together and covered them with sheets, and they had turkeys, hams, sweet potatoes, dressing, peas—everything that you could want to eat or drink—buttermilk, and tons of beer. In all my travels I have never seen a bunch of men pour down as much beer as those people did, and judging from the size of their beer bellies, it looked like they did it every day.

72

Still, they were as nice and friendly a bunch as you would ever want to meet; their dinner was for everybody in town that didn't have anywhere else to go, or friends to eat with. And that included us, because they really wanted us to eat with them, which we did.

I went back to the hotel and got the doctor because he didn't have anyplace to go, either, and so we all ate.

Then I'll be durned if it didn't happen again that somebody in there knew me. It was a guy who hadn't seen the game, but he'd heard about it, and that me and Jimmy D. were traveling with a hypnotist. He waited for us to finish eating, then he banged on a platter and got everybody's attention and introduced me as a celebrity in the house, the "kid from Joplin" who had beat Cracker Johnson out of $1,000 and made him give up in one game.

Cracker Johnson, I was beginning to find out, was kind of a famous pool player, and all of a sudden I had myself a nickname—"The Kid from Joplin." Jimmy D. started teasing me about it, but I couldn't help it. I liked the way it sounded, and I also thought he was a little jealous.

I ended up playing a couple of exhibition games against their two best players: an Irish guy named O'Donnell and a man who was wearing glasses so thick I wondered how he could even see the balls. I beat them both pretty easy. It was all for free, though, and so, like the doctor, we left town without making any money.

And that was only the start of it. Somebody knew about me in the next four towns we hit: Springdale, Harrison, Russellville, and Conway. So, what with schools still out and the doctor not making any money, and what with people in the pool halls knowing about me, we had everything going out and very little coming in.

We were getting pretty discouraged, but then in Little Rock we got a break. When we got to the pool hall, a place called the Brass Rail, the bartender there had known we were coming and had been sort of advertising the event. There was a huge crowd of people in the place and some of the people, you could tell, had ducked out of work to be there.

It was the first time anything like that had happened to us; we were surprised, and didn't know what to think about it all. Then the bartender, whose name was Daggett, took us aside and told us what was going on.

"I heard about you guys and saw the advertisement in the paper for that Polgart fellow, so I've been selling tickets to a contest between you and a man named Bucky Crouch, who's a lawyer in town."

"Are we playing for money," Jimmy D. asked him, "or are we playing for love?"

"How does $300 sound?" he said, and smiled what I thought was an evil smile.

Jimmy D. looked around and judged the crowd, listened to the cash registers going, and shook his head no. "Five hundred dollars, if we win—you put it up as a prize. Three hundred dollars right now or we don't play—call it an 'appearance fee.'" Win or lose, we had made our whole week's work.

Well, your honor, I don't know what kind of lawyer that Bucky Crouch was, but I do know what kind of a pool player he was, and he flat out beat me, fair and square. I almost never had a shot all game, and every time I took a chance and missed, he took advantage of it. He beat me 125 to 88 and won the $500.

Jimmy D. immediately offered him another game for that newly won money he had, but he wouldn't play and I didn't blame him; the money was in his pocket and he was going to keep it there.

"And that's what happens," Jimmy D. said when the doctor's show was over and we were on the road again. "You gamble around salesmen and they travel around and shoot their mouths off, and pretty soon you can't go anywhere where they don't know you."

It was the beginning of the end for us, not only with the circuit, but with everything.

After Little Rock we swung south through two little towns named Sheridan and Fordyce. In Sheridan, I remember, they were putting up their Christmas decorations and had a big tree on the courthouse square. The doctor did all right at the school even though it was still the holidays, but we couldn't do anything with our pool because the pool hall was over a shoe-repair shop that had moved out and turned off the heat. That's what it said on the door when we tried to get in, "No heat."

In Fordyce they had a pool hall, but it might as well have been closed. There was only one guy in it, and he had two broken legs.

I have to tell you about him because it's kind of funny. He was a roofer and was putting a roof on a church out in the country near where he lived. It wasn't a real steep roof, he told us, but he was still afraid of falling off, and so he tied a rope around his waist, threw it over the top, and figured how much slack he needed to get around. Then he looked around on the other side for something to tie it off to, but there wasn't anything, so he backed up his truck and tied it to the back bumper. So what happens is his wife comes by and sees the truck and gets in and starts it up. She doesn't see the rope, and he lets out a yell, which she does hear but can't figure out what it is. She backs up and dangles him a little first, then she takes off and whips him over the top.

And there he was in the pool hall with two broken legs. It would've been sad except the guy wasn't sad. It was an accident and he couldn't do anything about it, so why be sad, he figured.

Talking to him turned out to be almost like being in a

75

prophecy because it was that very night, with us on the road from Fordyce to Hot Springs, that we had an accident of our own.

It was the week before Christmas, beginning to snow, and we were all tired and just trying to get here. In all the traveling we'd done we'd never even come close to having a wreck, then all of a sudden there we were, on the last home stretch before the circuit was over, and Jimmy D. fell asleep at the wheel. I wasn't sleeping. I was sitting beside him on the seat watching the snow come down, sort of hypnotized by it, and listening to the radio, and then the road began to curve slowly to the right in a big sweeping curve and Jimmy D. just went straight. It was like everything was in slow motion. I looked over at him, and he was sound asleep. So I hollered for everybody to watch out, and we went through a little ditch and through a barbed-wire fence, and ended up out in a cow pasture under a tree with a bull looking at us.

The tree had torn off the luggage rack on top and our stuff was scattered all over the ground. We weren't hurt at all, just scared. The doctor was mad as hell, of course, since his car was all dirty and scratched up, and he was cussing Jimmy D. pretty bad, which he had a perfect right to do, except I was trying to warn him not to.

Right or wrong, Jimmy D. was not the kind of person to put up with that kind of stuff long; he calmly pulled out his pistol, which the doctor had forgotten about, and pointed it right between the doctor's eyes, just like the doctor said at the trial.

Nobody got killed in the wreck or after it, either. Jimmy D. squeezed off a shot just for the hell of it, but straight up in the air like he always did, and that was the end of the cussing.

We picked up our stuff and got it all packed again. My

suitcase was busted, but there was some rope for me to tie it together. The car worked, so we went on and nobody said anything to anybody about anything, but we all knew it was the end.

More when I can. Right now I've got to stop.

Sunday, October 24, 1948

Dear Judge Francis,

Your honor, as you can see, it has been three days since I last wrote because I just got worn out and I needed to rest my brain. I'm starting all over again because Mr. Harmon, my lawyer, has taken all my pages and has gotten them typed and has read them again. He says you are back in town now but you can't let me out until you know what you're going to do to me. He says you might not send me to prison, but that it depends on two things: on whether or not you believe my story and on whether or not you can find someplace for me to live.

Well, I'll keep trying to tell you what happened as truthfully as I can on the first thing, but there ain't anything I can do about the second thing. If I tell you something and you don't believe it, just ask me to prove it to you and I will. I have been practicing playing the harmonica, for instance, and can already play "Home, Home on the Range," and "From the Halls of Montezuma," and "The Whiffenpoof Song," which is the third one in the book I have, and goes, "We're poor little lambs that have lost our way/Ba, Ba, Ba." It doesn't make a lot of sense, but everybody likes it. If you don't believe I can play them already, all you have to do is ask me and I'll do it. If you don't believe that I'm a good pool shot, give me a while to practice and get my eye back and I'll play you or whoever you want.

The same is true of what I'm about to tell you next about Sidewinder Bates. Sidewinder's stuff is all packed and stored in Mr. Harmon's office because he left it all to me. The pictures are all there that I'm going to tell you about, and if nobody ain't stole the big headlight diamonds, they'll be there, too.

The same goes about my card playing and dealing; if you don't believe what I'm about to tell you, just bring me a deck of cards and watch.

So now I'm ready to go on.

When last I wrote, I wrote about Jimmy D. running off the road and getting the doctor mad. I guess the next thing I have to tell you about is Hot Springs and Sidewinder Bates, and what all went on between Christmas and June. Then I'll finally be ready to tell you about the gunfight, and how there wasn't anything else I could do but be in the middle of it.

First, Hot Springs.

It was two in the morning when we came pulling in, and the first place the doctor had us stop was the Chicago, Rock Island, and Pacific Railroad station. The station is almost in the heart of downtown, so what he was doing was giving us a choice: we could get on a train, or we could walk downtown and make some other arrangements. At any rate, the circuit was done and we were fired, afoot, on our own.

"I'm tired of you both," he told us. "I don't want to see either of you, ever again, and you—" He was about to say something nasty to Jimmy D., but Jimmy D. opened his coat and let the doctor see the handle of his gun, and instead the doctor just drove off, leaving us with our stuff on the platform, at Christmas, in a strange town with snow falling, and

I never saw him again until the trial, where he came to testify against me.

It could have been sad, except it wasn't. The doctor didn't drive too well even when it was dry, and he gave the car too much gas for the tires and went fishtailing all over the street. His friend, Ole Capt'n Jack, wasn't helping him much either. After he'd made it around the corner and was out of sight, we heard the crunch of a fender being crumpled, and smiled.

We spent the night right there in the station, sleeping on the benches, and in the morning washed up in the lavatory.

During the night it had gotten colder, and though the snow had stopped coming down, the stuff that was on the ground had turned slick to ice.

"We can't carry this stuff. Give me your suitcase and I'll go get us a locker," Jimmy D. said. He carried both suitcases back in the station and I waited for him, out there on the platform, liking the cold and glad that I'd broken down and bought myself a good coat. He was gone what I thought was a long time, though, and I was about to go look for him when this guy walked up to me and asked me if I was sick.

"No, I ain't sick," I told him. Then he started asking me other stuff. Did I have any trouble with my bones, or did I have rashes or flourishes of dizziness?

"I ain't got any of that," I told him. I thought *he* had to be sick or crazy himself to just walk up to people and ask those kind of questions, but he wasn't. He was trying to drum up business for a doctor in town who specialized in hot spring-water bath treatments, that was all. He was passing out handouts the same way I'd been doing for the last four months, and I wondered what else he might be up to. Down the platform there was another dude doing the same thing for another doctor, and that's what kind of town I figured I'd come to.

Finally, Jimmy D. came back. "Checking on schedules," he said, and handed me a key. "Had to get two lockers," he said. "Tried to save a quarter, but couldn't get them both in one."

We walked down a couple of blocks past a hotel that was so big it took up a whole city block of its own, and found ourselves on Central Avenue; then we steered north because that's where they had the Christmas decorations up and where it looked like the action was.

We passed a row of the fanciest-looking buildings I'd ever seen in my life, buildings with wooden curly-ques and carved stone naked women and grapes and birds. I thought at first that they might be houses of ill repute, but they weren't. They were places where normal people went and took baths, but it took me a while before I figured that all out.

Hot Springs, Jimmy D. was telling me, was a famous place. It was such a famous place that Woodrow Wilson had turned it into a national park, and tourists flocked to it by the thousands.

What they came to see, though, I could never quite figure out. The only thing unusual about the place was that hot water came boiling up out of the ground in places, and it was supposed to be good for you to sit in it, and that's why the dudes were down at the station drumming up business for doctors.

It was silly looking, but right there in the heart of downtown you could see people walking around in their bathrobes. In the summer there'd be lots of them, all over the hotels and in all the parks, in the stores and cafés, and even in the U.S. Post Office, which I always thought would be against some kind of law. In the winter there wasn't so many, but there were still a few. I didn't think I'd ever see it, but there were two old geezers in their bathrobes, with their shoes and socks on and garters holding up their socks, smoking cigars and playing dominoes in the pool hall. The pool hall was easy enough to find, as it was right there on Central Avenue, right across from another big, ten-story hotel.

I have to tell you about the hotel first because I was impressed. It was as big as the one we'd passed on the way down the hill from the station, and was shaped like a crown with two tall towers in the middle and two stories of pent-houses up there on the roof. The outside walls were made out of a light-colored brick that looked like pink marble in the ice, and there was a porch across the whole front of the building that was as wide as the street.

It was the Arlington, as you know, and that's the way it looked when I first saw it, like it was a magic castle or something, and looking at it made my stomach feel queasy, like I was hungry for something and didn't know what. I did know that it wasn't food.

Well, actually I *was* a bit hungry for food, too, since all I'd had to eat was a chicken salad sandwich at the snack counter in the station, and the chicken they'd made it from had been dead a long time.

Neither one of us was even halfway thinking about hustling pool; we were—or at least I was—thinking about what we were going to do next. Jimmy D. said he remembered a friend who lived in Hot Springs, a friend we maybe could live with until we found ourselves another circuit. He asked me if I minded waiting for him, and I said I didn't.

So there I was. I had about $50 in my wallet and about $1,600 in the cigar box in my suitcase at the station, so I wasn't worried. I got myself two cheeseburgers, sandwich-style with lettuce and tomatoes, and sat there relaxing and not paying much attention to anything, which is the very first thing Jimmy D. had cautioned me against doing.

There was this old guy who came in, I'd say 65 or so, dressed in a wrinkled old brown suit and regular brown cowboy boots and hat that were as old and worn-out looking as he was, the kind of old man you wouldn't look at twice, except he was real interested in me. I could tell by that time when somebody recognized me, and he did.

Sure enough, he came over to where I was sitting and handed me his calling card, which had his name on it in fancy letters, "GEORGE 'SIDEWINDER' BATES." He asked me if I was The Kid from Joplin, and if I was, did I want to play. His hair was solid white and his face looked like the skin on chicken feet. I didn't want to play him because I was afraid I'd beat him and he'd get all excited and croak on me.

But we played, and for $100. I told him I didn't have it on me to pay if I lost, but could get it without any trouble, and that was fine. He wanted to know how old I was, and I lied and said 16. Then he wanted to know about how I'd been traveling, and I told him about Jimmy D. and the circuit, and I ended up doing more talking than shooting. I hadn't had a chance to practice much over the last few weeks and so I wasn't on my best game. He, in turn, was excellent, and never tried at a ball he couldn't make. Calm as a man who'd been doing it all his life, he started running up balls and left me wondering how he'd done it.

During the whole game there'd been a guy in a chauffeur's black uniform—those short knicker pants and a round-looking little cap with a bill in front—watching us, and he had a big press camera and kept taking our picture. That got everybody in the pool hall to watching us, and I kept watching the door, hoping for Jimmy D. to come back so I could pay. I could tell I was going to lose and it was going to be embarrassing.

Well, to make a long story short, your honor, I lost. "I have to go up to the train station," I told him, and he offered me a ride in his car.

And that's how I met up with Sidewinder Bates, by losing $100 to him in pool. If I'd been on and won that first game, none of the rest of this would have ever happened.

Monday, October 25, 1948

Dear Judge, your honor, here next is how I got fixed up.

The old man's car was a black Cadillac, and had three seats just like the general's car that the doctor had. I couldn't believe it. The odds against riding in two three-seater cars in a row like that must be a million to one, but there I was doing it. It had to be a sign of something, I figured. I didn't know what it was I was supposed to do, but I knew something was coming.

The guy in the chauffeur's suit who'd been taking the pictures belonged to the old man, too, and he held the door open for us to get in and closed it behind us just like in the movies.

In the car, I asked the old man if he was rich, and he said, "Oh lord, yes," and that got me curious about something else. There was something about him that seemed familiar, something I couldn't put my finger on, so I asked, "Were you—" I didn't know what it was I was trying to say, "were you ever famous?"

"Yeah," he said, shaking his head like he'd been asked that same question a thousand times and it had always pained him greatly, "but not as much as I ought to be."

He might have said more, but we got to the station first. The afternoon sun, I remember, had melted all the ice and turned it back into slush; the chauffeur, whose name was

Randall, stepped out right into a big puddle of it that came up over his shoetops. You should have heard that man cuss. He came around, though, and held open our car door, then followed us inside. I wondered how much he got paid for that kind of stuff.

I found the locker my things were in and unlocked it, and there was my suitcase, except that it had been untied and was open. I held it closed and took it over to a bench, and there was my cigar box with all my stuff in it, except my $1,600, which was gone. What there was instead of money was a train ticket to Vicksburg, $40 in cash, and a note.

The note, and I still have it somewhere, said, "Hope this doesn't set you back too bad. Hate to do it, but I need it more than you right now. I.O.U. $1,600. Jimmy D. Watley."

The old man, Sidewinder Bates, had been fingering the stuff in the box while I read the note, and could tell what had happened. I tried to show him the note, but he didn't seem to care about it, or about the fact that I couldn't pay him what I owed. What he was interested in was the ace of spades playing card that had been in my mother's things. He picked it up and looked at it, and turned it over, and held it up to the light, and looked at it again. He even had *me* looking at it.

"I'll be durned if it ain't real," he said, and he pointed to the picture of the building on the back and said, "You know what building this is?"

I told him I didn't know.

"That's the old Palace Hotel in Denver," he said. "And this ace is from one of the decks of cards they used to use."

"Is it worth anything?" I asked him, thinking it might be valuable, a collector's item or something, and that's why my mother'd kept it.

The idea struck him as funny and he started laughing. "Worth anything? Not by itself. Not 30 years too late. But put two or three more aces with it and put them in the right hand and they could've been worth a fortune. They used to play for pretty high stakes at the Palace."

He wanted to know where I'd gotten the card, and I told him about Vicksburg and being an orphan and all, and he looked at me different from the way he'd been looking at me up to then. He reached out and took my chin and turned my face one way, then another, looking past my Dumas look to my real features.

"I'm going to ask you something terribly important, and I'd like for you to tell me the truth." We sat down side by side on the bench there in the station. "What were your father and mother's names, and what do you know about them?"

I got out the official documents from the orphanage and showed them to him. On the birth certificate it said "Father's name: Tobias Monk" and "Mother's name: Rose (Byrd) Monk."

"According to this, you're only 14½." The old man tried to act like he was disgusted, but I could see he was proud. "What did you go lying to me for?"

"I'm sorry, sir," I told him. "When I get the money, I'll—"

"You got a picture of your daddy anywhere?" he interrupted me.

I showed him the picture in the locket, and he looked at it and smiled.

"Randall," he said, "help get this boy's stuff together and take it out to the car." He put his arm around my shoulder and started walking me out. "I've got a better picture of your folks I think you'll like to see."

What I probably should have done, your honor, was take the ticket for Vicksburg that Jimmy D. had bought me, trade it in for one to Memphis, and start fresh from there. I felt like I knew Memphis because I'd been delivering its newspapers and reading them all summer. I knew more about Memphis, really, than I knew about Vicksburg.

But I didn't; I went with them to look at the picture of my folks he promised, because where else could I see something like that, and the next thing I knew I was caught up by that old man the same way as Br'er Rabbit got caught up in the tar baby.

Back down the little hill we went, to the same place we'd left from, except instead of going back into the pool hall, we pulled up to the Arlington, the big hotel I liked so much. The black Cadillac and Randall were owned and employed by the hotel, not by Sidewinder Bates. Sidewinder was just one of their permanent guests—one of the old folks who lived there all year long and got special privileges and paid special rates. He was also, I found out, some kind of shareholder, and worked for the hotel off and on, but I'll tell you about that when I get to the pictures. Right now I want to tell you about the hotel itself, because it was a whole new world for me.

We walked in the lobby, and it was like getting hypnotized. Everything was polished and expensive and just right and big. They had green plants growing in the middle of winter, palm trees, and the pots they were growing in were like the ones in *Ali Baba and the Forty Thieves;* if they'd been empty you could've curled up in them and hid. They had three pianos that I could see; they had a floor that was so clean it looked like you could get right down on your hands and knees and lick it.

Sidewinder began introducing me to people, and as he did, it got worse and worse. He introduced me to the people at the main desk and told them that I was his friend and guest, and he got me a key to his room. Then he told the overall manager, whose name was Gulley and who seldom got far from his office and ledgers, that I was going to be his guest for a while. Then he told another man, whose name was Riley and who was the *concierge* (which was a new word for me and meant that he was the person who really ran the hotel) that I didn't need money—all I had to do was just sign my name and get a copy of the bills.

Riley wore a fancy red velvet coat with gold braid on the shoulders, and had a gold key around his neck. He was about as snooty a person as I had ever seen. What Riley did was look me over, frown at how I was dressed, and wiggle his nose. It was Riley's job to be snooty and look down his nose at people, I found out. It gave the hotel some flair.

From the lobby on, it was like I was floating, except I wasn't. The carpet was so thick it grabbed at my ankles and made me pick my feet up too high. It was like walking in slow motion.

"A week from now you'll know this place like you know your old shoes," Sidewinder promised. So now I was not only his old friend who was going to be his guest for a while and who could have anything I wanted just by signing my name, now I was going to be staying for weeks. . . . I have to tell you the truth, your honor, I thought the old man might be funny (if you know what I mean by funny), and I was ready to bust him upside the head and start running at the drop of a hat. I mean, there I was, going up in an elevator to his rooms to look at some pictures he had promised me he had of my folks. If he showed me the wrong kind of pictures, he was going to be sorry.

Now I'm sorry I was even suspicious because it wasn't like that at all. We went up on the elevator to the eighth floor, and his rooms were like a regular apartment, smaller than what you'd find in a house or apartment building, but fancier.

There was a living room in the middle, a kitchenette and a tiny bedroom on one side, and a tiny office and a big bedroom on the other. The living room was the biggest room, and had couches, a pool table, and a bar. The office had a desk, bookcases, file cabinets, a telephone, and pictures all over the walls. The tiny bedroom, which had my suitcase sitting in the middle of the bed, had a double bed and a window that looked out onto Central Avenue, and a tiny little bathroom and shower.

"I hope you will stay with me awhile," he said. "There's everything you need here, and you wouldn't be any trouble to me. The maids come and clean up, and when I'm hungry I just call down to the kitchen and tell them to send something up. If you're worried about me, you don't have to be. You'll see why I'm doing all this when you see the pictures," he promised. So we shook hands and I agreed to stay.

I liked my bedroom and could have lived in it forever; there was a closet, and a desk and chair, a mirror, a clock, and a radio. Sidewinder had to dig through his files and find the pictures he wanted me to see, so in the meantime he ordered us something to eat and drink and I unpacked, took a shower, which I was dying to do, and scrubbed my stinking feet. Whatever kind of fungus Jimmy D. had had on his feet, I now had on mine, and mine smelled worse than his. I was afraid that if Sidewinder smelled them, I was going to be back out in the cold.

I'll have to stop for a while and write you more tonight.

Monday night

When I came out of the bedroom, Sidewinder was standing waiting for me at the bar and had two little glasses ready. I went over to where he was, and he poured a drink of whiskey for us both. That's the way he drank whiskey, poured in a glass like they did it in the old days, standing up at a bar. Whiskey, he liked to say, was special, and that's the way you ought to treat it.

"A toast," he said, motioning for me to pick up my glass. "Here's to Comanche Bill and to the son of Tobias Monk. . . . To the old days, and to the future, which I feel better about already."

Well, I looked at the label on the bottle and it wasn't Ole Capt'n Jack, so I drank it. After Jimmy D., I half expected the old man to shoot off some kind of gun, but he was more civilized, and didn't. Jimmy D. was wild, and one of a kind.

"That's Comanche Bill behind the bar. Ever hear of him?"

Behind the bar was a painting of a chestnut-colored horse, a racehorse of the old-fashioned kind, and there was his name on a gold plate on the bottom of the frame. He looked like he ought to be famous, but I'd never heard of him at all. I'd heard of Assault, War Admiral, Whirlaway, Count Fleet and, of course, Jet Pilot, because he'd just won the Kentucky Derby that spring, but I hadn't heard of Comanche Bill.

"Well, he won some big races in his day, and I sold him for a lot of money. It's Bill who pays the rent, so he gets the place of honor and I toast him every day. . . ."

He poured himself another toast, but not one for me, and toasted him again.

"Sold him, in fact, to Al Capone, who got mad at him for losing the Kentucky Derby, I heard, and ate him."

For some reason, that struck me as funny. I knew how Al Capone looked from seeing his pictures in the newsreels, and how his mobsters looked. The idea of him and his mobsters sitting down at a table with bibs around their necks and knives and forks in their hands, wearing those funny gangster hats and eating poor old Comanche Bill seemed like the funniest thing I'd ever heard in my life. First I started laughing, then Sidewinder got to laughing, then we were both almost rolling on the floor.

One of the things I've always liked about people, your honor, is their sense of humor, and Sidewinder Bates's was about the best in the world. He liked laughing and making people laugh, just like an entertainer on stage, which I guess in a way he was.

It took a while, but finally we got our senses back, and when we did, Sidewinder's mood had changed. It wasn't like he was unhappy, but more like he was sad or his feelings were hurt.

"I'd give everything I own not to be old," he said, "to be just starting out like you are." He looked so sad and lonesome I thought he was going to cry.

And so we were both sad together for a while, and then the mood shifted again. We were still sitting at the bar and then I noticed that he was over being sad and had gone into a trance. It was like some memory had taken over his mind, like he was hypnotized or something. I was used to that sort of thing and knew there wasn't anything I could do about it, so I just waited till it was over. It only lasted a few minutes, then he was back to normal.

"I get ghosts," he said, shuddering like people do when cats walk over their grave.

Finally he remembered what he'd promised me at the station.

"The pictures," he said. "I promised you pictures, didn't I?"

And right here, your honor, is where I found out what I had gotten involved in.

We went in his office, and all over the walls, as high as you could reach standing on a chair, and right down to as low as you could see sitting down and bending over, there were pictures from the old West. They were pictures of people, mostly—cowboys and miners, and women and men in wagons, but there were some pictures of buildings, too, hotels and places made out of canvas and boards that were frontier saloons. There was one picture that was bigger than all the rest, and it was framed the best and in the best place, which was on the wall right behind where Sidewinder sat at his desk.

"That's me and Wyatt," he said, and by Wyatt, your honor, he meant none other than Wyatt Earp. You could tell it was real, and hadn't been doctored up or anything. They were wearing suits and vests and ties and were standing in front of a building called the Great Northern, and under the picture it was printed, "Wyatt Earp and one of his dealers in front of the Great Northern." It was printed in that white print you see on old pictures, like it had been a postcard and Sidewinder had had it enlarged. You could tell, though, that it was the real McCoy. There was even the name of the studio that had taken the picture, the place, and date: "Butch Rogers Studio, Nome, Yukon Ter., 1904."

On one wall there were pictures of Sidewinder doing lots of things: playing cards, on a horse, getting his boots shined, working on a gold claim, drinking with people at saloon bars, all of them taken back in the old days. Then on another wall there were some more modern pictures of him wearing fancy suits and posing with people even I could recognize. There was one of him and Babe Ruth, and one with Al Capone, and one where he was on a big speaker's platform out in front of the Arlington with Eleanor Roosevelt.

He had scrapbooks, your honor, with pictures in them like you wouldn't believe. He went through them page by page, showing me pictures and saying things like "Here I am in 1905 in Goldfield, Nevada, where I owned an interest in this place. . . . Here's an outside shot . . . and here's Wyatt again . . . and this is a good one of Bat Masterson and Wyatt and me at the Jack Johnson–Jim Jefferies fight in Reno . . . July the 4th, 1910, it was . . . and here's Tex Rickard," who did such-and-such, and so on.

Finally, there was the one he wanted me to see, one that had been taken in front of the Silver Exchange in Virginia City in 1922. It showed Sidewinder and a young man and woman, all standing and smiling and facing the camera. Sidewinder and the man were holding up a bag of something that could be silver, gold, or just plain money, which they looked happy about. The woman was dressed in a fancy dress and bonnet and was carrying a parasol.

"That's your father, Tobias Monk, and your mother, whose name back then was Rosie Byrd. They weren't married then, but they were thinking about it. We were partners for a while in a dance hall called the Busy Bee. Gambling was illegal by that time, which meant it had moved to the back rooms, but it still went on, and Toby Monk was one of the best at it I ever ran across. . . . You can see we were doing all right because of what you see us holding."

My father was taller than him and, I was happy to see,

didn't look like a Dumas. He was in the middle of his 20s, it looked like, and had a big mustache but was already starting to get bald. My mother wasn't very pretty; in fact, she wasn't pretty at all. She was dark-complected and her hair was dark and as thick and spongy-looking as swamp moss. I thought it was black, but Sidewinder told me it was brown and almost pure red in certain light, and that it was the prettiest hair in town. She had what I thought was a pretty big nose, and so did I, so I'd say of the two of them I looked more like her than him.

Sidewinder went on with his story. "I never heard anything about you, because you were born long after I drifted out of Nevada. I went back to Virginia City in 1928 or '29 and heard that Toby'd had some bad luck—that he and Rose had gotten hitched and had a baby, but that the baby had been killed in a mud slide, and that he'd lost his place because it had burned down mysteriously, which meant he'd been caught in a reform movement, and that he had given up gambling and gone back East somewhere. That was the way it was back in those days, you knew everybody who was on the frontier and in the gambling trade. You could be partners with somebody one month and with two or three others the next month. You could win everything and have people working for you, then you could get cleaned out and be working for them. . . ." He shrugged his shoulders like it was all he could say.

But it was enough, and if he'd have told me any more I don't think I could have heard it anyway. My head and heart were already so full of pleasure that they couldn't have stood any more. I wanted to tell somebody, but I didn't have anybody to tell and so was about to just burst.

All those years, your honor, of people telling me that I was no good, and of being an orphan and being too ugly for anybody to adopt, all the time not being able to argue or fight back because I never knew who I was or who they

95

were—there's no way you can imagine it till it's happened to you. Then all of a sudden you find out you're somebody, not nobody like they tried to make you out to be.

I'll tell you something, your honor, there wasn't too many kids in the home like me, kids who couldn't remember their parents at all, only five or six of us, but we all had the same nightmare—that we were the sons of somebody terrible, axe murderers or something like that.

It made Sidewinder happy to make me happy, and he gave me that picture. He also sent it out with Randall to have it enlarged and framed, and he hung it on the wall in my bedroom. In fact, we started a whole new picture collection just for me, and it was that one, the picture of me with the pool cue in Joplin, which he had gotten from the pool supplies salesman, and one of the ones Randall took of Sidewinder and me in the pool hall across the street, those three, they were the start.

Tuesday, October 26, 1948

Dear Judge Francis, your honor,

I want to thank you for coming by the jail this morning and talking to me about my case. I didn't know Mr. Harmon had sent you my story already, but I'm glad he did and I'm glad it was what you had in mind for me to do. It's easier for me to pretend like I'm talking to you now because, in a way, I am.

You say you want me to tell you all there is to know about Sidewinder Bates; well, I'll try, your honor, but it won't be easy because it's going to take forever, and you said you want to make a decision on me next week. It helps to know that you know about poker and used to play a little yourself when you were in the army, because that's what Sidewinder was, a professional poker player.

It would also help if you could read the book that Sidewinder was writing. He had the idea that gamblers were the most important people who ever lived and was trying to show how if it weren't for gamblers like him and me, nothing would have ever happened. Because what were King Ferdinand and Queen Isabella doing when they backed Columbus with ships if they weren't gambling, and what was Columbus doing when he got in his boat and started sailing but gambling that the world was round? If it weren't for people gambling with their money and their lives, this country would still be waiting to be discovered.

And he had a good point, your honor. Even people who didn't agree with him to start with ended up agreeing with him. I have seen him get after preachers and do-gooders and have them admitting all sorts of things.

Even the Bible is full of stories about gamblers, he would argue. For instance, what was fishing if it wasn't gambling, he would start out. You couldn't see what was down there under the water; one place looks just like another place, so all you can do is just throw in your nets or lines and close your eyes and cross your fingers. Then this guy comes along and acts like he's got some inside information, or like he knows where the fish are, and he says, "Fish over there on the other side of the boat."

So you take a chance and do it, and you catch fish and make a little money for your family. You go to the track to bet on the horses and it's the same thing. All you're trying to do is make a little money so you can feed your family. Say you don't know nothing about fishing, all you know about is horses, and this guy says, "Bet on number seven."

That's what it was like to argue with him, and it's all in his book. So read his book, your honor, and you'll get a good idea of how he thought about things.

Now, I don't think I've spelled it out what he had in mind for me, but here it is: He wanted to make me into a big-league poker player like he was, and he wasn't going to spare anything to do it. His book was not only going to be a history of gambling, it was going to be the story of his life, and I didn't know it at the time but I was going to be his last chapter.

The first week or so I was with him, he took me places and bought me things he said I needed. "A gambler can't be a regular person; he's got to be special, and that means he's got to dress special," Sidewinder would say, and every day there was someplace to go and somebody to see—a tailor, a bootmaker, somebody.

So pretty soon I had a whole new wardrobe, and I'm not talking about the kind of stuff you see in stores. He bought me what he called "gambler's outfits" and paid enormous amounts of money for them. Boots—he got me three pairs of them, black, brown, and a fancy pair of gray alligators that had pure silver tips covering the toes. Pants—I had pants of every color you could imagine, even a peach-colored pair that I hated to wear because they made me look like I was buck naked. Shirts and vests and coats—I had them with lace all over them and with fancy Western piping and fringes; I also had a buckskin coat just like the kind that Roy Rogers sometimes wore, only mine was better.

I had two suits that I'd wear when we had to get really dressed up: one with a white coat that was called a dinner jacket, and one with a black coat that had tails in back that hung down like feathers.

Every morning I would have to shave, whether I needed to or not, especially my mustache, which was beginning to thicken up, and I'd have to use after-shave lotion because women liked it, and women were important.

There were places he wouldn't go without having women with him, and he had three or four who were pretty enough to be models or movie stars who he would call to be our companions for the evening. It was all most proper, your honor, and we never diddled with them, mainly because he was too old and I was too anxious.

"Besides," he would say, "it's work, and you don't confuse work with pleasure."

The places we would go were the gambling casinos, which I'm sure you know about, and what he wanted me to do was study what went on, and he was right, it was exactly like work because there wasn't any fun in it. We'd come in the Cadillac with Randall driving us, with women in gowns and furs hanging on our arms, and we'd go in and act like big spenders, shaking hands and buying people drinks—not me, of course, Sidewinder did all the glad-handing and back-pounding; I would just tag along. The manager of the club would take us around, and we'd join some parties that were going on in the banquet hall or in the nightclub; we'd pose with fat cats who had pretty girls of their own at their tables, though not as pretty as ours, and Randall would have his camera out and be taking pictures. On a night out like that, we might have had our picture taken 10 or 20 times, I'd get introduced to maybe 100 people, and Sidewinder would expect me to remember every one of their names. When we'd get back to the hotel after the night was over he would quiz me on them, just to see how good my mind was, and I'd be able to get about half.

But, going on with our tour of the club, after we finished meeting people and shaking hands, we would take a slow stroll through the game rooms and watch the play for a while. Roulette was always busy, and so was a game they played with dice in a cage called chuck-a-luck, and black jack. The crap table would always be the fullest, and sometimes there'd be people two deep just waiting for a chance to play. Randall took more pictures, but he wasn't allowed to use flash because it was too much of a distraction and made people nervous.

What we would do was this: The next day we'd have the pictures and could study them, and Sidewinder would point out things like who was winning, how much, and why. Then we would look at pictures we'd taken the week before or two weeks before, and there they'd be, the same people winning again, and Sidewinder would start teaching me stuff. A guy named Greasy was a chipper, which meant he'd help people haul in their chips when they won a pot and palm a few chips in his hand. Another guy was named "The Genius," and what he did was memorize cards in blackjack. He never won a lot of money because if he did the club would get tired of him and run him out, but he always won

It got to where, your honor, pretty soon we'd go out on a visit to the clubs and I could just walk through and see everything that was happening. And I'm not talking about a long time, I'm talking about five or six weeks. I don't think many people could have learned as much stuff as I did as fast, but in my favor I had the time I'd spent in the pool halls with Jimmy D., and I had Sidewinder always there to keep me on my toes.

Like I say, to us it was work, but that's not the way it looked in the newspapers when we got in the shoot-out. The papers showed me and him with the women and the dinner clothes and furs and drinks everywhere, and they made me look like I was pretty worthless, a playboy who belonged in prison.

Which is what most people don't know about gambling—that if you do it right, it ain't fun but a lot of hard work.

Every day, your honor, Sidewinder made me read four newspapers; did you know that? The Hot Springs *Sentinel*, the Arkansas *Gazette*, the Memphis *Commercial Appeal*, and the St. Louis *Post-Dispatch*. If we were going to visit somewhere out of town, say to Atlanta, we'd start reading the Atlanta newspapers, too. Every day we'd have reading sessions, and he'd show me things in the paper I'd missed.

And most people don't know that Sidewinder was really working for the casinos we visited. He got paid for being there and putting on that celebrity act, and Randall sold copies of the pictures he took to the clubs, who gave them to their biggest customers and to losers as souvenirs of their good times. Sidewinder Bates had a purpose for everything we did, and I do mean everything.

All of this is why it's so hard to tell you about Sidewinder Bates. Look at what I've told you already, and I haven't even gotten to poker or the good stuff.

So let me change the subject a little. I couldn't say this at the trial, your honor, but I've always believed down deep, deep, deep in my heart that there's something wrong with gambling, something I couldn't put my finger on and still can't. I told Sidewinder about it, and he blamed it on my mother.

"There's something about gamblers," he said. "We walk down the street and people turn to look at us; we tell people what to do and they do it. Children want to grow up and be just like us, and a woman will fall in love with us at the drop of a hat. She will be married to some honest, hard-working citizen for years, and somebody like you or me can come to town and turn her head with a single look. What we are is what she wants—adventure, romance. And if we tell her to, she'll leave her honest, hard-working-citizen husband in a second and follow us anywhere."

We did most of our reading and talking, back in those days, while we ate breakfast in our rooms. Breakfast came up with the morning papers at seven sharp, and we seldom got up from the table before eleven. I liked eating in the room best because when we went out to restaurants, Sidewinder went back to teaching me things, like how to order from menus in French, and how to order Chinese food, and on and on, because, like reading the newspaper, that was part of the gambling, too. When we went out to eat, people, especially women, kept turning their heads to watch us.

"The trouble is," he went on, "the minute they get their hands on us, the first thing they want us to do is quit. Quit gambling. Settle down and play house with them. Become honest, hard-working citizens just like the poor dudes they just left. Don't ask me to explain it," he would shake his head, "because I can't."

And he was right, your honor; I have a lot of my mother in me, and so while Sidewinder was pushing me in one direction, part of me was not wanting to go. I remembered people like that war hero in Louisiana whose money I took, and I remembered others who wouldn't have played against me if I hadn't tricked them into thinking I wasn't as good as I knew I was. I have what a good poker player can't afford to have, or even let in the same county with him, and that's a guilty conscience.

I told Sidewinder that, but it didn't faze him.

"I've got a plan," he said, "and when I'm done with it, you'll be done with your conscience."

Now, there's one last thing I have to tell you about that nobody knows but me. I'm not a psychiatrist or anything, and I can't say for sure, but I think George "Sidewinder" Bates was as crazy as they come. I don't know the name of the kind of craziness he had, but what is it called when you think you're Napoleon (and I'm not talking about being hypnotized)? What is it when you think you've been sent to Earth with a mission, or you've got this special ghost of a person living in you who tells you what to do?

The last thing I want, your honor, is to say anything bad about Sidewinder Bates, who I love like a father, and I wouldn't even say this now if I thought it was bad, but Sidewinder Bates was as crazy as a loon.

Tuesday night

Dear Judge,

I just read over what I wrote this morning and it seemed like everything was too serious. It wasn't all work, my learning to be a gambler; we also took time out to play, and had fun doing it. One of the first things I did, when my boots didn't kill my feet so bad, was walk up to the top of West Mountain. I didn't know that was what I was doing, but that's the way it turned out.

It was after Christmas and things had warmed up a little. I just started walking one morning, and I went across Central Avenue because I wanted the morning sun at my back, and I started going uphill. Then the hill got steeper and steeper yet, and it made me mad. It was like the durn thing was laughing at me, daring me to keep going. Every time I'd get to the top of one street, there'd be another steeper one; it went on like that block after block.

Then, finally, I won and was on the complete top. There was a park up there and an observation tower, which I wasn't mad at and didn't need to climb. I could already see everything I wanted to observe from where I was. I could see the top of the Arlington, and I could see all of Central Avenue and figure everything out. Hot Springs was built in a gorge between two big mountains, the one I was on and the one I could see right across the way. I couldn't tell for sure, but it looked like the hot springs all came out of the other mountain because that's where the fancy bathhouses were. North on Central were big houses and stores; to the south were the railroad yards and the race-track. It was so clear that morning I could even see riders and horses.

About a week later I escaped again and went for an afternoon walk. I climbed up the other mountain, North Mountain, but I did that one on purpose. That time, though, I got caught in a cold, sleety rain and thought I was going to freeze to death. It was as cold as a penguin's pecker, and half the way back down I had to scoot on my bottom because if there's one thing cowboy boots aren't good for, it's walking downhill on concrete and ice.

I thought Sidewinder was going to be mad because he'd had it planned for us to take a ride up to Little Rock and meet somebody named Percy, who was going to show me something about the gamblers' supplies he sold, but there wasn't any doubt I was going to be sick.

Instead of being mad, he called downstairs to the bathhouse that was in the Arlington and told them I was coming down, and to give me the complete treatment.

And oh, your honor, I thought I was going to die from the pleasure. There were two big-shouldered women there to tell me what to do and I did it. I got out of my clothes and there was a long, skinny towel to wrap around my bottom, and they gave me something to drink that I think now was a shot of brandy, and now I could kick myself for not finding out if it was the kind Napoleon liked to drink, and I got into one of the tubs that had the hot spring water running through it, and them two women pulled curtains around me and just let me soak for a while.

And then I knew why people thought hot water was

good for you and cures things. It cured me of just about everything, I think.

When I got out, they poured hot oil over me and gave me a massage, and I'll swear they were reaching down into my back and wrapping their fingers around my bones. Finally there I was, an hour later, going back up through the hotel in my robe, just like the people I thought were dingy when I first hit town. Now I was dingy, too, and glad I was.

After that I tried to get down to the baths as often as I could, which surprised Sidewinder some because he didn't think I would like them.

But I like most things, your honor. Once at a fancy French restaurant he had me order something that turned out to be snails. I ate them and liked them, and he was surprised at that, too. He didn't know that when you were raised in an orphanage you tend to like everything. And once he had me order something that turned out to be calf's brains, and they were delicious, too. After that it got to be a contest, and I always won. You put something on my plate, your honor, and if it smells good and tastes good, I'll eat it.

We also went to movies, though I went more often than he did because he got stiff when he sat too long.

It's funny, and I haven't thought about it at all till now—I certainly didn't think about it at the time—but one of the movies we went to see was the one called *My Darling Clementine*, and it had Henry Fonda in it playing Wyatt Earp. That was later on, in March, I think, because it was before my 15th birthday, which was in April. We went on our first tour in May and the shooting happened in June. I think now that that movie must have sat on Sidewinder's mind like a time bomb waiting to go off.

When we came back he went into another one of his trances.

And that's because of all that O.K. Corral business. I'll be telling you about all that when I get to it. Right then I didn't know any more than you do now, and I have to stop now because Mr. Jackson is blinking the lights.

Friday, October 29, 1948

Dear Judge, your honor,

They took the wire off my teeth and checked them to see how they were tightening back up. Now I've got regular braces that look ugly. They would look funny at a poker table, but I don't guess I have to worry about that much here. I'm eventually going to have better teeth than I did before I got hit, they say. They won't stick out so much, and if you had anything to do with them getting fixed, I thank you.

I haven't seen Mr. Harmon, my lawyer, in three days now and I'm beginning to worry that he's gotten wrapped up in his new case and has forgotten me. But I know that isn't so and that I'm only imagining things. If he were here, he'd just say go on and write.

So that's what I'll do. And what I need to tell you about next is Sidewinder's plan to get me started in gambling. I told you about his wanting me to be the last chapter of his book. Well, it wasn't enough to wear good clothes and look like a gambler; for me to be a gambler, I had to learn to deal, and play, and cheat at cards.

It wasn't like one thing happened and then another thing happened and so on; everything I'm talking about was happening at once. While we were out going around buying clothes and showing off at the casinos, and while we were reading papers and keeping up with the world, we were also spending about six hours a day sitting at the table in the kitchenette with a wool blanket stretched over it to give it the right texture for playing cards—draw poker, stud poker, and something called low-ball, which I hated but which I had to learn to play anyway because other people liked it, and it always came up in games of dealer's choice.

I've never seen it fail—you ask somebody how they learned to do something and they'll say, "the hard way," which means, I guess, that they learned by doing it wrong till they got better. Not me. I can say that I learned to play poker the easy way, from a professional who was just like a schoolteacher who'd give me tests and quizzes and traps to fall into, and who'd get mad as hell when I fell into them. He wouldn't cuss me exactly, but he'd call me some pretty terrible things.

"Boy," he'd say, "I've seen bowling balls that know more than you. What do you mean betting $50 on a pair of sixes?" I'd say I was trying to bluff him out and he'd just shake his head. "You don't bet $50 on a bluff to win $30 in the pot. Do you know why?" I wouldn't know why and he'd have to tell me. "Use your head. You wouldn't bet $50 to win $30 if you had something good; when you do it on a low pair, you're telling everybody you're bluffing; you might as well just announce it over the loudspeaker." And he would be disgusted with me and give me bad looks till I did something right to make up for it.

He'd give me $500 to play on, and we'd play till he won it all back; then he'd go over what all I was doing wrong till I understood it. After that he'd let me take a break and think about it, or we'd go shopping for something; then he'd give me the $500 again and we'd start all over.

What it takes some people a lifetime to learn, with Sidewinder's teaching and hollering I had down in months. It started with him winning the $500 back with no trouble; then it got harder and harder, because, dumb as I was starting out, I learned fast. January, February, and March, all through the winter months, three hours, six hours, sometimes nine hours a day he'd have me at that table in the kitchen, practicing to be a gambler.

And that's the way it was, day after day, except that's still not all of it. On top of everything—I told you it was hard work—I had to do exercises. One kind of exercise was to keep me from getting fat because I was sitting around a lot and eating a lot, and if I didn't do something, my new clothes weren't going to fit. I was doing push-ups and sit-ups in my room, and swimming downstairs in the pool, and taking steambaths and hot baths at night, and doing sit-ups again before I went to bed.

The other kind of exercises he had me doing was to help my fingers. I had a piece of string and a book on cat's-cradle tricks, and I practiced making string figures, some of which were pretty complicated, like Jacob's Ladder and the Apache Door. When I wasn't doing that, for at least 30 minutes to an hour a day I practiced shuffling in front of my dresser mirror, which was beveled so I got front and side views, just trying to see if I could get a glimpse of a card.

Because if I could see a card, then you could bet that Sidewinder could see a card, and you could bet that he'd tell me about it. "The eight of diamonds is on the bottom," he'd say, for instance. "Sure hope you don't need it."

Then I'd practice cheating, and I had a book with pictures in it showing me step-by-step how to deal "seconds," which means keeping the cards on top and bottom where they are and dealing the ones next to them. That meant more time at the dresser watching my hands in the mirror to see if I was being too awkward.

Which I was. But then Sidewinder, when he told me to study the book, never intended for me to learn to cheat.

What he wanted me to do was see how cheaters did it—how their hands worked, how they held the deck and dealt—so when I was playing in a real game I could take care of myself.

At first it was Sidewinder and I who'd play at the table, then he began inviting people in from the hotel staff. Cooks, dishwashers, bellhops—he'd pay them by the hour to play; they'd get to keep what they won and he'd give them back the money they lost. So there was never a lack of people wanting to play.

It was amazing. Sidewinder had taught me thousands of things about playing cards, and drilled them into my head till there they were, and one day it all seemed to sink in and make sense, and I started playing poker like he wanted me to. I knew what people were going to do before they did it: raise, drop, bluff, or just hang on and hope. I can't explain it because a lot of it happens in your mind. When I knew it was time to take control of a game, I just did it and not even Sidewinder could beat me.

Sidewinder had been trying to teach me to do everything right—dress right, act right, have the right manners, and play poker right—to think and act like a professional gambler, which I was very soon going to be.

The whole first part of his plan was coming to an end, and I'd be lying if I didn't say that I was tired of doing the same thing over and over, and ready for something new. Considering everything, where I'd come from and how comfortable I was living, you wouldn't think it was possible, but, nice as it was, I was getting awfully tired of that hotel.

It was April—spring—my birthday month. On the day that I turned 15, Sidewinder called our women companions and we went out on a birthday toot, singing and dancing and just generally having fun. It was a full-blast party without any work involved except getting our pictures taken a few times. It was the second time I'd ever drunk champagne, and I drank too much of it too fast for my own good.

One of the places we went was called the Clubs and Diamonds, and you might remember a picture the district attorney showed the jury of me sitting at the table with champagne bottles in front of me and my hat turned sideways on my head and my eyes all glassy. That picture, your honor, was one of the ones that was taken that night, and it made me look terrible, but it didn't tell the truth.

I felt so bad the next morning that I swore off of drinking altogether and haven't had a drink of anything with alcohol in it since. You've got to do it once, else you don't know what you're up against, and that's what Sidewinder wanted me to find out. If I were a father and had daughters, I'd get them drunk and teach them how to keep from getting taken advantage of. I'd feel guilty if I didn't.

Luckily, I could go back to sleep and spend the afternoon in the baths, and I lived. But even after I lived, after the party and the hangover, I was still ready for something new to happen, and Sidewinder was ready, too. My birthday present from him was a trunk.

It was a travel trunk, a big one, the kind that I imagine people used to take on trips around the world. It sat on its side and opened from the middle so that it was like a traveling wardrobe. Outside, it was steel with brass covering the seams and corners. Inside, it was covered with green silk and there were rods to hang suits and coats, and compartments for things like underwear and socks and cuff links and such. There was a place in that trunk for everything you could need, even a compartment which was a tiny medicine and sewing chest. There was a drawer that was full of gambling supplies: chips, cards, and a rule book by Hoyle. Sidewinder must have been planning to give it to me for a long time, because there were train-schedule booklets, fingernail files and clippers, a pair of binoculars, an umbrella, a compass, and a shoe-shine kit.

I told him I loved it, and he said, "Let me show you the best part."

When the trunk was all folded up and locked, right under the right-hand hasp there was a secret panel. You opened it by pushing down on the middle of the hasp and pulling out the pin in the hinge it turned on. The panel opened up and there was a small compartment inside, and in the compartment there was a $1,000 savings bond, which was issued in my name, and a gun.

It was a silver-plated, pearl-handled .38 derringer that wasn't much bigger than a deck of cards. It was loaded and ready to go, and holding it in my hand reminded me of holding a tamale, it felt that slick and delicate.

Sidewinder had his own trunk, smaller, but just as fancy as mine, and he'd had it hauled up from the storeroom in the basement. "It's time for us to take a trip," he announced, and he handed me an envelope with round-trip train tickets to Memphis. The second part of his plan was for me to go with him and see what goes on at a big convention.

Memphis. After reading about it forever, at long last I was going to see it.

Saturday night, October 30, 1948

Dear Judge, your honor,

I tried to write some this morning but was sick and dizzy and couldn't think straight. What I was going to tell you about was the trip to Memphis, so here goes.

Traveling with Sidewinder was a lot better than traveling with Jimmy D. and the doctor because Sidewinder always went first class. To Memphis we traveled by train instead of by car, so there wasn't going to be any wrecks, and at night we had our own sleeping compartment with our own beds, and I slept like a baby the whole way.

In the morning, while we were traveling through what I thought were rice fields, we sat at a table in the dining car and had breakfast, eating off of real china and with silver knives and forks—eggs and biscuits that had been cooked right there on the train. We were all dressed up in our best gambling outfits, and we must have looked special because two young women came giggling up to our table wanting us to autograph our names on pieces of paper for them. They were twins, they said, and they'd just gotten married and were on twin honeymoons. Autographing things didn't bother Sidewinder at all, but it sure enough made me feel guilty.

Then we got into the station and took a cab to our

hotel. It was bigger and better than the Arlington. The lobby alone was so big that you could've put a good-size three-story building in it. There were shops and restaurants, banquet halls and meeting rooms everywhere, and you got the feeling that there was more going on in that one lobby than there was in the whole state of Arkansas—except baths; they didn't have any hot spring water baths.

What they did have, and to me this was really something, was a television set. It was hard to get to see it because there were always so many people around it. If you weren't in the first two rows or tall as a giant, you couldn't see it at all, but I slipped in low and saw a little of it. It was sort of like a big radio and a little tiny picture show all mixed in one, and what was on while I was watching was some kind of show where you looked at this pair of eyes, and they gave you about 15 or 20 clues and you had to figure out who the eyes belonged to. Everybody who was watching was guessing and arguing and wanting to bet they were right. I was worried for a minute that there was going to be a fight. It was a little bit like the jackpot game at the Elks Club in Vicksburg; a man drew names and telephone numbers out of a drum and called people till he got somebody at home who made a guess. If they guessed wrong, another 50 dollars went in the pot and they gave you another clue.

And it seems to me, your honor, that people keep doing the same things over and over and over again. In a way it's even funny.

But back to the convention and what we were doing. Outside all the meeting rooms' and banquet halls' doors there were billboards saying what was going on in those particular rooms and when. Mostly it was events that had to do with the convention: in a place called the Rebel Room, all afternoon there were going to be new mortuary products on display. In the Steamboat Room there were lectures and

115

demonstrations of new mortuary techniques. At the time, I didn't know what "mortuary" meant and wasn't paying much attention to the people the hotel was full of.

In front of all the elevator doors there were more billboards, all advertising the Skylight Room, which was up on the roof and was a nightclub. There was a picture of the band that was going to play that night. The picture had a fat man with a clarinet in his hand and a grass skirt around his belly. There were fake palm trees and a fake ocean and a beach. He was in the middle of a bunch of pretty girls all wearing hula skirts and making a big to-do over him. He had a fake bone that was supposed to look like it went through his nose and he was grinning and eating a chicken drumstick. According to what it said, he was the "King of Bongo-Bong," and I wanted to slip up to the roof that night and see him more than anything else in the world.

We got checked into our rooms, and Sidewinder gave the bellboy some money and one of his cards. "Give this to your hotel detective and ask him to call me," he said, and the bellboy, who wasn't a boy at all but an old man, looked at the card and smiled, and gave Sidewinder his money back. It seems like years ago the old man had been down on his luck and Sidewinder had saved his life with a $200 tip. Things like that happened all the time with Sidewinder.

"When you're going to gamble in a hotel," he said, "you either pay off the hotel or you end up paying off lawyers. The hotel is usually cheaper." And then the detective called, and we went downstairs to have a meeting in the concierge's office.

It turned out that they both knew him, and that was another thing: Everywhere we went we seemed to run into people who either knew Sidewinder or knew about him. The house detective was a man named Casey who knew him because he had once been a gambler himself and played in a game with him. The concierge knew about him because he

116

knew all about the Arlington. Both of them said they thought Sidewinder'd retired.

"I have," he said, and then the subject got to be me and how Sidewinder was teaching me the business.

Well, pretty soon Sidewinder had the use of one of those meeting rooms, one of the smaller ones that didn't have a special name, and his own billboard outside it.

Sidewinder and them discussed what he wanted to do, and the arrangements were agreed upon. Sidewinder was going to give a short lecture on the partnership of the Western gambler and the Western undertaker, and that would make him part of the convention. Then he was going to demonstrate techniques that gamblers used to cheat, and teach the undertakers how to detect them. Then finally, immediately afterward, for a buy-in fee of $500, whoever wanted to try their skills against an authentic Western gambler would have the opportunity to play in a "demonstration" game. In return for the price of their buy-in fee, they would be given $500 in poker chips, which they could use in the demonstration game.

It was a legal way of saying what was illegal to say, and it worked. I didn't know what the Western undertaker part had to do with anything because I still didn't know what "mortuary" meant. I didn't figure that out till Sidewinder started working on his lecture and I got to go exploring.

A convention, I found out, was something like a professional trade fair, where everybody who's in the business gets together and compares notes. Salesmen who sell the kind of supplies that the professionals use are there to show off their wares and take orders.

So, completely ignorant, I go down the elevator and get off on the first mezzanine, and there I am in front of the Rebel Room. It's afternoon and the display has started, so I go in and the first thing I notice is that all the windows are covered with heavy red velvet drapes, and all around the walls, painted right there *on* the walls, are pictures of the great Confederate generals on their horses going off to war: Robert E. Lee, Stonewall Jackson, Nathan B. Forrest, and some others I don't recognize. It's too dark in there if you ask me, but nobody asks me. The salesmen who are setting their stuff out on tables don't seem to mind, and then I see what they are setting up and it's OH LORD JESSIE! It's coffins and racks of suits and dresses with no backs and table after table of big needles, the kind they use to give shots to horses. Those people are selling embalming needles and funeral supplies, and I'm talking about some pretty awful-looking stuff—saws to cut dead people's heads off and hammers to beat things back into shape and big pliers to break arm and leg bones and straighten them out. The worst tables of all, though, are the tables where they've got real dead bodies and pieces of dead bodies laid out where you can look at them and feel how well they're all preserved.

It all gave me the creeps like I'd never had them before. I was out of there in less time than it takes me now to tell you about it, but I still get dreams about it all, and in my dreams I see those generals riding, galloping, and I know I'm dead because I know they're dead, and then all those salesmen see me and start chasing me. I try to get away, but there's nowhere for me to go and I wake up all in a sweat.

Anyway, that did it. I knew I wasn't going to go explore the Steamboat Room and listen to any lectures about embalming people, so I went outside and started exploring downtown Memphis. Mainly what I did was walk up to a park and buy some cotton candy and watch people feed pigeons. Then later on I walked down to the Cossett Library, which was a big red sandstone building that I recognized from the papers, and sat on a wall and watched the boats on the river. A hundred years ago, I remember thinking, that was where the gambling was, out there on the river. I had been around Sidewinder so long I was thinking like him.

When I got back to the hotel, Sidewinder's lecture had started. On his billboard outside he had put up pictures from his collection, pictures of him and Wyatt, and him and Bat, and him and Doc Holliday. Inside he had about 30 people sitting down in chairs listening to a story about the time in Leadville when the undertaker himself had died and there wasn't anybody around who wanted to bury him.

"The reason was," he said, "it was so cold. We had had a hard freeze and a sleet, and the undertaker, a man named Henry Tuck, had left instructions that he wanted to be planted next to his brother, Sherman Tuck, in the Tuck family plot, which was in a little town over in the next valley about five miles away.

"Well, so we took him over, all the gamblers in Leadville, Colorado—nobody else would do it—and tried to open a hole, but the ground was too hard. We hacked at it with shovels, with picks, and finally with axes, but it was like chopping at concrete in downtown Moscow.

"Then somebody thought of dynamite, and knew where to get some at one of the mines, and went to get it. We all had brought bottles of whiskey with us, it being so cold, so we started drinking and having a merry old time while we were waiting. Then the dynamite came and we stuck it in the ground and set it off, not knowing if the dynamite would work, and so using plenty. Well, it worked; it broke open the hole all right, but the problem was, we used too much and blew old Sherman Tuck right out of the ground.

"Then it started getting dark, and it started looking like snow again, and there we were with a problem. The funeral was going to be in the morning, so we got lanterns and we worked hard all night, trying to get everything back together again so nobody would know what had happened.

We did it. We got it all looking good around there again, and it snowed and covered everything up real nice; the next morning we had the most beautiful six-foot hole that you've ever seen in your life.

"We were going to get away with it, it looked like, but at the funeral the preacher got to talking too long, and one of the aunts was gazing off into space and happened to look up in a tree, and said, 'Ain't that the green suit we buried Sherman in?' And sure enough, up in the tree was Sherman Tuck."

Sidewinder waited for the people to start laughing, but there wasn't even a hint of a smile. Undertakers, I found out, never smiled. It was unprofessional for them to smile. They wore black all over and drove in black cars and they never, ever smiled.

"OK," Sidewinder went on, "that was the partnership between the gambler and the frontier undertaker: we killed people and you guys planted people, except every now and then you guys got to plant one of us, and every once in a while we got to plant one of you. Now let me show you some of the reasons people got planted. . . ."

And from there he went through a speech about the different ways people cheated at cards, and he showed them the same kind of cheating tricks he'd been teaching me. I could see him dealing seconds and from the bottom, but they couldn't. Pretty soon he had about 10 of them really interested, and of those 10, seven were willing to put up the $500 and play, for which they got to have their pictures made with George "Sidewinder" Bates, and got their own signed copies of the pictures of him and Wyatt, Bat, and Doc, pictures that Sidewinder just happened to have dozens of, right there with him. Of the seven who played, one even managed to win a few hundred bucks. Sidewinder himself cleaned up about $3,000, which wasn't a bad day's work, really.

"Now I want to ask you," he said to me, "those people I won the money from—were they happy or sad?"

I had to admit that they were happy. They were undertakers and they weren't smiling, but they were happy. You could tell it from the way they kept shaking Sidewinder's hand and looking at the pictures over and over, and how they kept talking about what they were going to do with their own pictures when they got them. None of them could wait to get back home and start practicing the new cheating techniques and using them on their friends. There was one guy who was sure his brother-in-law had been cheating *him*, and he was going to put an end to that.

"Right," Sidewinder said. "The money doesn't mean a thing to them; they'd lose it again gladly, and in fact they want me to come back next year. One of them told me I made him feel like he was important. Can you imagine that? Important! I did them all favors."

And that, your honor, was all he'd wanted me to see: how it was possible to gamble without feeling guilty. And I saw it and took it to heart, but it wasn't all I'd seen in Memphis, though, not by a long shot.

While the poker game was going on, for instance, I slipped out for a while and took the elevator up to the top floor to see what that nightclub act was like, and it was just like the picture, except that what the picture was of was a song number, like in the movies. I don't remember all the words, but the chorus went: "There ain't nothing in the world that I can't do/I make the laws and break them too/Because I'm the king/Yeah I'm the king/Of Bongo-Bong."

And the next day, for instance, we sent the trunks ahead and walked to the station through Beale Street. The photographer from the hotel that Sidewinder had hired for the night before went with us and I got my picture taken with a famous Negro gambler in a club called the Morocco, which was on the third floor of an old building that was so rundown on the outside you wouldn't think it could be as fancy as it was on the inside. Three times on the way up, even though they knew who Sidewinder was and trusted him, they stopped us and searched us for guns, and I saw how if you weren't careful, you could get yourself killed.

Sunday, October 31, 1948

Dear Judge,

Everything I have to tell you from now on has something to do with the gunfight and how I came to be involved in it, which is what you said you most want to know. In a way it all started back with that Wyatt Earp movie I told you about, but in another way it had its start long before I came along. I can't say for sure, but I have my suspicions.

You will also remember, I hope, how I wrote that Sidewinder wanted to take me to Little Rock, where he wanted me to meet a man named Percy who ran a gambling supply house, but I got caught in the cold, sleety rain on North Mountain and got sick. Well, I finally got to meet him on our way back from Memphis, since we had an hour's layover there in Little Rock and Percy's business was only a block from the station.

When I say "gamblers' supplies," your honor, I'm not talking about cards and dice; what I'm talking about is crooked cards and crooked dice. Ol' Percy was a master at shaving and marking cards, and shaving and loading dice. If you liked to cheat by wearing eyeglasses that had special lenses to see marked cards, he had the glasses and marked the cards. He could load you a pair of dice that you could throw all day and never lose with, or win with, depending on what you wanted, and even the experts couldn't tell they were loaded.

His real specialty, though, was cold decks, and if you don't know what a cold deck is, your honor, I'll tell you. It's a deck of the kind of cards that they use at a club or casino where you're playing—say, Bicycles, or Bee's—that come already stacked for the dealer to deal. All he has to do is make two or three fake shuffles and pull-throughs, and give the deck a cut and crimp so that when he gives the cards to the guy on his right for cutting, they get cut back just the way he wants them.

Say you're a crook, your honor. Say you know you're going to play in a club that has picture-backs; say it's a picture of a horse. You get a sample king, queen, or jack, a joker, and the ace of spades, and you take them or send them to Percy and he fixes you up with a few of his specialties. Most of the time you don't even have to send samples; he knows the club and the kind of cards they use. You pay him $50 a deck and you go play. You get into the poker game at the club and you play for a while, easy, letting somebody else win. Then, when you see where all the money is, you wait till it's your deal and you slip in the cold deck. You deal the big winner four kings or four aces and yourself a small straight flush. In that one hand you wipe him out and take all the money in the game.

The sinister thing about that kind of cheating is that it doesn't just wipe people out, your honor, sometimes it destroys them. They believe their hands are so good they bet money and things they don't have and can't afford to lose, and sometimes the losers kill themselves, and sometimes they go to jail.

So what kind of cheat uses a trick that rotten? When Sidewinder first told me about it, I pictured a real rat, with bad breath and sharp little teeth and a cheesy mustache, but that wasn't so.

"You'd be surprised at who my customers are," Percy told me. "For the most part, they're just regular people like postmen and car mechanics and shoe salesmen who play on weekends or paydays. They don't mind winning the money, but what they really like is wiping out their friends."

Now I have to tell you about Percy and his place because it'll help explain why what happened happened.

In front it was a newsstand and novelty shop, the kind of place that sold every brand of cigarette made and souvenir junk like little bales of cotton that said "Arkansas" and little-boy dolls that when you squeezed them they peed. There was some good stuff, though, like miniature Coke and 7-Up bottle cigarette lighters, and a collection of brass knuckles and pocket knives. My favorite things were little telescopes that you could look into and see a naked girl. I wanted to buy the whole box and send them home to the guys in the orphanage, but of course I couldn't.

Percy was about Sidewinder's age, or maybe a little older; the surprising thing about him was that he was married, and his wife was as old as he was and worked in the store right there with him. Her name was Shirley, and she had a white mustache and hair growing all over her ears and was as deaf as a brick. She could read lips, though, and do sign language, and Percy put her to watching the front while he took us on a quick tour of the back.

And the back was a different story. The first thing I noticed was that Percy also had a picture of him and Wyatt, taken in Virginia City, framed and hanging on the wall above his rolltop desk, and I was beginning to wonder what was going on. What did Wyatt do when he wasn't getting his picture taken, I wondered?

Percy had somebody who worked for him in the back room, somebody named Big-ears Baker whose ears were so little he almost didn't have any at all. What he had, though, was good eyes, and could see to do the fine work of running the tiny little drill that drilled the holes in the dice. It was Big-ears that showed me around and let me try out the merchandise. Percy and Sidewinder had gone in a storeroom for a secret meeting.

What that meeting was about, I've since figured out, was a favor or something Percy owed and Sidewinder was there to collect on. I think it was at that meeting that Sidewinder found out about the Paradise Lodge and the Luster brothers. Now what they actually said I have no way of knowing, but I think when we left to head on back to Hot Springs, Sidewinder's plans were already complete.

I remember, on the way back I laughed and said, "I think everybody west of the Mississippi must've had his picture taken with Wyatt Earp," just meaning to be funny and make a joke.

But to Sidewinder it wasn't funny. He had that look on his face, the same one I'd seen and told you about earlier where he said he had ghosts. "Never laugh at what you don't understand," he said, and then he said this, which I thought was strange: "People took pictures of Wyatt because he was famous; he knew it and liked it and let them do it. They took his picture because he *was* Wyatt Earp. They take mine now because I *knew* Wyatt Earp. There's a big difference."

"But everybody treats you like you're famous," I told him. I hated to see him looking as sad as he was.

"Wyatt has made me a wealthy man," he admitted. "I've made a hundred times the money he ever did, and lived in a thousand times the comfort. . . . Still, it's not the same."

And that was the trouble with history, he told me: The wrong people get remembered for the wrong reasons, and the right people get forgotten.

"But I'm not done yet," he said, and he had a look on

his face that was as cold as some of the ones I'd seen on the gravediggers in Memphis.

That's all he said about Wyatt Earp and the subject of history for a while, but that wasn't the end of it.

More this afternoon.

Sunday afternoon, October 31, 1948

Dear Judge,

Here it is afternoon already, and my writing fingers are still sore from this morning. I keep telling them that there's not much left to write and they keep not believing me. As you can tell, though, I am getting close.

The last thing, of course, is my version of the gunfight, but before I get to that I have one final, and I do mean final, thing to tell you about, and that is the last trip Sidewinder and I made together.

The reason I have to tell you about it is because it was during that trip that I began to notice that something was on Sidewinder's mind, something he wasn't telling me about.

The first thing I noticed was that he kept putting more and more of the business of traveling on my shoulders. He had me make all the train and hotel reservations, telling me stuff all the time about how to go about it, what trains and hotels to choose and why. I was also put in charge of our trunks, and of seeing that they got put on the trains and ended up where we wanted them.

Second of all, the trip we were on was a swing around the West, through some of his old "stomping grounds," he called them, out through Denver, down through Austin, Texas, back through Biloxi, Mississippi, and home. To see the old places again, that was one of the things old people liked to do before they planned to die.

His purpose of the trip—and I had to figure it out for myself, he didn't just sit down one day and tell me—was that he was looking for friends from the old days. On the way to Denver he did tell me all about a man named Packy Davis who used to wait tables with him, back when they were only 10 years old, and usually ended up working for nothing because they lost everything, time after time, at the faro tables. When we found poor Packy he was in an old folks' home and couldn't remember too much. Sidewinder had hoped to take him back to Hot Springs with him, but that wasn't possible.

After Packy, Sidewinder didn't tell me who he was going to see because every one of them was turning out to be sad. He didn't have to tell me, though—I could see it in his face every time he went out visiting and came back. All of his old pals were either dead or too stove up to come back to Hot Springs with him, though I was curious as to why he would even have wanted them to. They would just be somebody else for him to have to take care of.

(Now I know why, I think. Wyatt Earp had his old-time friend Doc Holliday there at his side when he needed him; I think in his mind Sidewinder was looking for the same kind of thing.)

But back to the gambling and teaching part of the trip. He had me taking over so many things, he even wanted me to start keeping the records in the personal records book he'd been keeping for over 40 years. I started keeping up with everything—where we went, how we went, what it cost, where we stayed and how we came to stay there, who we had to bribe, and so forth. All of that was part of the business, and so were people's names. I had to keep up with the people who ran the hotels and the casinos and gambling games, the people I played cards against and their playing habits, and, of course, how the game went: who won, on what, how much, and how. The last thing I had to do before I went to bed at night was bring the record up to date.

That kind of stuff was important because things didn't just happen once, they happened over and over again, and once you had it in your records, you could go back to it. The undertakers' convention in Memphis, for instance—they've been meeting in Memphis the third week of April since 1902, and they'll keep coming back forever because they need to get away from their wives for a while and play a little poker and, as much as undertakers can, have a good time.

I think Sidewinder really did want me to be a gambler or else he wouldn't have gone through so much trouble. Here's what we did on the trip:

It was the first of May when we left town, and our first stop was Kansas City. There was a special train we had to catch, one called The Chief, because the association whose convention we were going to visit was making a film on board and they wanted me and Sidewinder to be in it.

The film was going to be called *A Vacation in God's Country,* and it was being made to advertise dude ranches in the Rockies. It was going to be the kind of junk they put on in picture shows as a short when the main feature isn't very long and they want you to feel like you got your money's worth. It was the sort of thing that was going to be boring and hokey and you were going to want it over with and the real show to begin.

Our parts were to be our regular selves. They had us sitting at a table in the club car playing two-handed cards when we get joined by two fat dudes wearing tight cowboy shirts and even tighter pants and who want to play. The announcer says, "You have to be careful who you play cards with on trains. Here's two innocents about to lock horns with the legendary Sidewinder Bates and his deadly young assistant, Dumas 'The Monk' Monk. Poker's the game, and we'll check back on this situation later."

Then it's "later" and we've got a big pile of chips in front of us and the announcer is supposed to say, "Oh-oh, it looks bad for our two Easterners, but the night is still young." Then it's even later than "later" and Sidewinder and I are out of chips and all we have on are our long underwear, hats, and boots. Our parts end when one of the dudes wins another hand and you see us starting to take our boots off and the announcer is supposed to wrap it all up with "All's well that ends well," or some kind of crap like that. I thought it was all pretty embarrassing and hope I never have to see it.

It was the Rocky Mountain Dude Ranch Association that was having the convention, and Sidewinder gave his talk about what it was like in the old days, except this time I helped him by doing the trick dealing, and he put his billboard out again, except this time my pictures were mixed in with his, and that night at the poker game I started playing first to warm everybody up, and Sidewinder came in to finish them off. I was supposed to lose a little, and I tried, but losing to those guys wasn't easy. They all had pretty bar girls, wearing those little fringed skirts and floppy blouses, hanging on them, and they cared more about those girls than about the money they were losing. In my first game of poker I played for exactly two hours and won $800, which was a fortune for me, but nothing to them. When Sidewinder finished with them, they had lost $6,000 more.

And just like in Memphis, they were still happy.

Sidewinder was right about one thing: There were lots of people who were willing to give up their money just to be happy and for a chance at being around famous people. "How many people," Sidewinder asked me once, "would pay $1,000 to play in a real game in Yankee Stadium?" I had to admit that I would.

"Millions," he said. "And that's the way you've got to think, like you're Yankee Stadium, because that's what I'm going to make you."

And there it was again, the plan he was working on.

When all the dude ranchers pulled out, we had a couple of choices. We could stay right where we were and wait for the next convention to begin and Sidewinder could try to find more of his old friends up there, or we could go on down to Texas and try the fishing down there. The next group scheduled for Denver was a bunch of highbrow college teachers, and Sidewinder was of the opinion that they were worthless. "They don't like to do anything but sit around and talk," he said, "and they've got the emptiest bunch of wallets you ever saw in your life." So we decided to move on to Austin, which was the next place Sidewinder wanted to go looking for friends.

And looking through the back years in Sidewinder's ledger for the second week in May, one of the interesting things we found was that that was the week the Texas State Legislature got together for its spring session, and, as you know, Austin is where the state capital is. The first thing the legislators did when they all got together, Sidewinder assured me, was party and gamble.

"Now there's where we'll find the fat wallets," he said, "and about the worst poker players God ever put on the face of the earth, if you can call Texas 'earth.'" Sidewinder hated Texas and everything about it, though I never knew why. I guess he felt the same way about it that I feel about Oklahoma, but he still had lots of friends there.

It was a long, flat, hot, and boring ride to get there, and the best hotel in Austin couldn't compare with the ones in Denver or Memphis or other cities—the elevators were always out of order and there was a smell in our closet that was like bug spray. The food was good, though, and I've always cared more about food than anything else.

In fact, I've decided that if I ever get out of jail I'm going to learn to cook. Everywhere I've been there's been something special that the people like more than anything else. In Louisiana it was shrimp. In Oklahoma it was steak, but they cooked it too much, so they don't count. In Memphis it was pork that they cooked real slow in brick ovens and called bar-b-que. In Denver it was trout. We went to a restaurant in Denver where they had live rainbow trout swimming in a tank in the front window. You picked one out and sat at the table and 30 minutes later you were eating it, with its head still on and its ugly eye looking at you. In Austin, and all over Texas, it was chili and Mexican food, and I could talk about Mexican food all day, but I'm getting too far off the subject again.

I just wanted to say that there's more things in life than gambling, and I was beginning to figure some of them out, even back then, and I'm not just saying it now to try to get out of jail.

Yankee Stadium. Didn't I tell you that Sidewinder was crazy?

In Austin he started doing something in private that he never did in public: he started running down Wyatt Earp and Bat Masterson and even Doc Holliday, who he barely even knew. It was a little bit like biting the hand that fed you, I thought, because, as Sidewinder had said himself, Wyatt Earp had made him rich.

"Wyatt was a terrible gambler. The only reason he had any money at all was because of his partners. All he was was a name. . . ." It was strange hearing him talk about those kinds of things after hearing him talk so much the other way.

133

"Earp was never much of a lawman, either. His brother Virgil was. . . . Had twice the guts that Wyatt ever had. . . . The lawmen who nobody wanted to mess with in Dodge were the men like Ed Hogue. Wyatt had a fancy gun and was all show, but he never seemed to be around when the shooting started."

Imagine how different this all was to me.

"He killed one drunk in Dodge and got fired for getting in a fistfight with the mayor, and that was it. Then he went out to Tombstone because Virgil was the marshal, and together they could pick the miners clean. One fight he gets in, one fight in his whole life, the one at the O.K. Corral, and he's famous for it forever—a Western legend. Let me show you something."

We were in our terrible hotel room in Austin and were unpacking at the time, and he pointed to one of his pictures of Wyatt; in the middle of Wyatt's tie there was a stickpin that had a diamond on it as big as a pearl.

"Those things were called 'headlights,' and the reason gamblers wore them was to brag on how good they were; the bigger the headlight, the better the gambler. So it was the last thing they wanted to part with."

He made me take a good look at it, and so I did. Then he opened the secret compartment in his trunk and took out a jewelry pouch and dumped it out on the table.

"Wyatt had 13 headlights, and he lost them all. Here're three of them I won myself."

And he had, your honor, three of the biggest diamond stickpins I'd ever seen in my life. He wore one and I wore one that night when we played against the state senators. I started first and won over $2,000; those guys were doing things like betting hundreds of dollars on two low pairs; you won't believe it, so I won't tell you what all they did, but Sidewinder was right, they were the world's worst.

Sidewinder knew a lot of them, and they even played

worse for him than they had for me. He and I played 16 different people in all, with more waiting to play when the game broke up, and I don't even know how much money they lost, but it was considerable.

If we could have kept going around and could have kept playing and winning like we were doing, we'd have made more money than the president of the United States ever thought about making.

After Austin, nothing in Sidewinder's ledger and in the papers looked promising, so we decided to be tourists and went over to New Orleans, where I really got to thinking about food seriously, and to Biloxi, where Sidewinder finally gave up looking for old friends. Mississippi was dangerous for me because I was a fugitive, but I didn't know it, and since I didn't get in any trouble, neither did anybody else.

Biloxi was a big gambling town where there was lots of action, but the play was between the kind of urchins that hung out in cheap casinos and took advantage of bad amateurs, and the amateurs were all innocent recruits from Keesler Field. They came into town on 24-hour passes with their paychecks and would lose $20 or $30 to the slot machines, roulette wheels, or blackjack tables, and go back broke. It was pathetic, and everything smelled like dead fish, but they called it fun. I had a girl come over and sit in my lap and call me her lover boy. It surprised the devil out of me.

Finally we decided to head back home, and got on the train that was going to take us there. It's amazing, but there I was, almost a year later than when I first moved in, going by my old bedroom in the Rhodus garage. It was eight at night when we came through the yards, and I could see a light in my old bedroom window, and there were cars locked up in the bullpen waiting for the owners to come pay the fines. It made me feel funny to see it.

Well, that's the end of it. That's the whole story, as much as I had time to tell, about what all I've done and what-all has happened to me so far, and how I came to get in the fix I'm in. The rest, I guess you could say, is history, and the die was as good as cast.

And that's because when we got back to the Arlington, there was Jimmy D. sitting in the lobby waiting for us.

Monday, November 1, 1948

Dear Judge, your honor,

My lawyer, Mr. Harmon, now has everything typed to here and is waiting for this, he says, because today is Monday. He wants to get this typed and get it to you by Wednesday morning because next Monday is the start of deer season and he says you are determined to do something with me before it starts because the legal system sort of shuts down till it's over.

I will try very hard and finish my story today or tonight, as I can understand about deer camp and have always wanted to go to one myself. There was one out in the woods behind the orphanage, right there on the Big Black River, where you couldn't swim in the summer because it was so snaky but in the fall was pretty nice. The kids in the home used to go out to climb trees and watch them hunt, and they looked like they were having a lot of fun.

The last thing I told you about was getting back to town and finding Jimmy D. waiting.

I'll start right there, with the charge that Jimmy D., Sidewinder, and me were all three in on everything right from the start, and were all three equally guilty of manslaughter under the eyes of the law. Jimmy D. and I didn't have any idea what Sidewinder was planning. As far as

Jimmy D. was concerned, he had just showed back up in town because he was broke and was hoping I could refinance him again. When he got here and found out I had fallen on good times and was off traveling with a millionaire gambler, he decided to hang around till I got back.

Now I think Sidewinder looked him over and could see what kind of person he was in a second—it probably didn't even take that long. And you would think they wouldn't be the kinds who'd hit it off, but they did. They smiled and shook hands like they'd been knowing each other all their lives, and Sidewinder asked him if he was hungry, or needed anything right away. Other than a little spending money, Jimmy D. said he didn't. He had a room in a flophouse up the street.

On the elevator up to our rooms, Sidewinder said, "Jimmy D., you look like you could handle yourself in a fight. I'm not wrong about that, am I?"

I could almost have guessed how Jimmy D. was going to answer that. Instead of answering, Jimmy D. pulled his coat back and let Sidewinder see the handle of his gun.

And like I say, I knew something was going on. Now all of a sudden, it was starting to get clearer and clearer what Sidewinder was planning. When we got up to our rooms, Sidewinder wanted to talk to Jimmy D. alone, and sent me on inside. What Sidewinder and Jimmy D. talked about out there in the hall, again, I don't know, but I think Sidewinder gave him some money, maybe even $2,000 or $3,000, knowing how Sidewinder worked, and told him to hang on at the flophouse for a few days, because that's what he did.

After that first day, I didn't see Jimmy D. for a while. I spent the next few days catching up on the entries in the records book and looking ahead at likely places for my own first trip. But this is what I know went on:

Jimmy D. bought a car, a little Chevy coupe with a rumble seat, and Sidewinder got him a job with a beer company who took beer around to all the places in town that sold it, including the Paradise Lodge Resort out on Lake Hamilton, which had a golf course and a place where you could dock your boat, and a big gambling joint that they called the Paradise O.K. Corral.

Your honor, if they hadn't named that place that one particular name, I don't believe anything bad would have ever happened, but they did, and to Sidewinder it was like a red flag waving in his face.

Car . . . job . . . then what? Then Sidewinder and Jimmy D. drove up to Little Rock, visited that gambling supply house—that little weasel named Percy—and came back with a carton full of what I now know to be cold decks. What they also did sometimes during that first week was to go out to the Paradise Lodge and lose a little money; three days in a row they did that, going each time without me, and coming back each time and not answering my questions.

This is what I knew for sure; this is what Sidewinder finally told me, and what he asked me to do.

He got Randall to take us up to the top of West Mountain, and we climbed up to the top of the fire tower, which for him wasn't easy. It took us forever since he had to take the stairs so slow. There wasn't anybody up there but us, and the view was nice, so it was worth it, I guess. It was as close to heaven as Sidewinder figured he was ever going to get.

The sun was shining, the sky was pure blue, and the wind was blowing those little fat white clouds around. Looking down on Hot Springs with the leaves and grass such a bright green, it looked like a View-Master slide with brand-new batteries.

"There's an outfit in town that we're going to hit," he

said, and he told me about the place for the first time. "They've been cold-decking people for years, I know that for a fact, and it's time somebody put a stop to it.

"Now it doesn't have to be us," he said, going on, "but why shouldn't it be us? If you're going to be a special person, you've got to do special things. Jimmy D. and I are going out there tonight and give them something to think about. What I'd like for you to do is go with us and do the playing."

Right away I was going to tell him I'd go, but he held up his hand to keep me from saying anything. "Wait and hear it all. If you go, you'll have to take your gun, and if you take it, you might have to use it. You might get killed, though I don't think that will happen, and you might have to go to jail for a while, which is more likely."

I was still going to say I'd go, but he wasn't through. "You should also know the rest of it. I'm dying. Ain't no doctor told me when, but I know it's coming, I can feel it in my stomach, and it's time for me to start thinking about how I want to go.

"With Jimmy D. it's another story. This sort of thing is fun for him, and I know what he's like better than he does. A hundred years ago he would've ruled the West. Now he's just trapped, and unless another war breaks out real soon, he's doomed. But you, you've still got everything ahead of you."

"I want to do it," I told him, and he put his arm around my shoulder and gave it a squeeze. "History," he said, "is finally going to give us a chance."

I think he truly believed that sometime in the future, people were going to make movies about his and my life the same way they were making them about Wyatt's and Doc Holliday's. He was going to be the new Wyatt, and Jimmy D. was going to be the new Doc, but I wasn't real sure who I was going to be like. There wasn't exactly a part for me all that mess.

This is my side of what happened.

The plan was I was the one who was going to sit in on the game and play, and that's all I had to do all night, just play cards like I'd normally play cards, nothing fancy or dangerous. I'd get my share of winning hands and my share of losing hands; I was to just take them as they came.

And that's what I did.

It was going to be Randall's job to drive us, and to take along his camera to get pictures in case of trouble. According to Sidewinder, there were so many versions of the original O.K. Corral fight that there was no way of knowing what actually went on. "But just think of what would've happened if they'd had a camera."

And I *have* thought of what would've happened. Everybody would have the pictures and look at them, and *still* argue about what went on; at least that's what happened with us.

So we got out there a little before eight, because that's the time the poker games got formed up, and I bought my way in with $2,000, got my chips, and sat down. Sometimes the place had two or three games going, but this night there was only one. There were four players already at the table, and they were testing their luck before everything got started by high-carding for $5. One man was down $45 and the game hadn't even started yet.

Now, I'd say the people at the table th_____ were pretty good poker players. One guy wa_____ up at Fort Chaffee and had cleaned out_____ other man, a tall, skinny guy _____ than me, the one they ca_____ mistake all night; th_____ kept getting second-best hands. He'd get a jack-high straight, say, and I'd have a queen-high. The third guy at the table could play all right, but he had other kinds of problems. First of all, he couldn't see. His eyes kept blinking closed constantly, and even when they were open they didn't do much more than squint. The poor dude once stayed to the end of a seven-card stud game trying to catch a diamond flush when, if he could have seen to count the cards, he'd have seen that all 13 diamonds were already out. It cost him $350.

The last two to sit down at the table to play were Harvey and Zack Luster, the Luster brothers. They ran the game for the Paradise Lodge investors, who lived all over the world and didn't care about anything but money. It was the Luster brothers who were the crooks, and it was them we were going to put out of business.

There were three other people we had to watch out for, though. There were two bodyguards who stood right behind the Luster brothers' chairs, Jim Pat Reynolds and Swifty Smith, who looked like they'd been in a thousand fights and lost them all. They both looked like they'd been stomped, cut, scalded, dragged, and gouged at one time or another. It was hard to look at them in the face. The third guy we were watching out for was the floor boss, a mean little man who was covered with hair and was named Shaw.

Of the three, Shaw was going to be the most dangerous, Sidewinder figured, because he wasn't playing or guarding anybody; he was walking around free, and if trouble broke out, you wouldn't know where he'd be or what he'd be up to. It was like chips, who brought things to the tables, like drinks, when the play most importantly, like new decks of cards That was the for them.
scribed in court back to where and that's the way everything was

Between eight and ten,

the games just went like games normally go. Then, some time after ten, I began to win bigger and bigger pots. The Luster brothers were getting more and more new decks, Zack Luster especially, and what they were doing was using me to clean the other players out. The first one to get in trouble was The Birdman, and then it was the sarge, then old squint-eyes. Their places got taken by other players, and things went along neutral for a while again. . . . I guess I was $2,000 or $3,000 up. Then I hit another big hand and cleaned out one of the new guys—$4,000 up, plus my own $2,000 that I'd started with. I had $6,000 in chips altogether, and that's when Sidewinder decided that we'd quit for a while and go get something to eat. The Luster boys didn't like it much, but they didn't know what to do about it either.

We left Jimmy D. sitting at the bar in the corral and walked over to the big lodge and ate steaks, knowing that when we went back to the game, we could expect a showdown.

"They'll want to raise the price of poker," Sidewinder said, and that was all he said.

Everything in me wanted to say, "We could just quit, you know," but there was no way I could've said it, so I just ate. I felt like there wasn't a thing in the world I could do about what was going to happen.

The steak was tough and was fighting me back, and I couldn't do anything about that either. We looked at each other, I remember, and he didn't care any more about eating than I did.

"You know, they say the reason old people c⸺⸺ at night is because they've done so many bad ⸺ lives, their consciences won't let them." ⸺ steak with his fork and pushed it awa⸺ reason, my conscience doesn't hu⸺

because I never got old." Then he smiled and said, "When all of this is over, we're going to be so hungry we could eat a horse."

"Comanche Bill?" I said, and we tried to laugh a little, but it was really kind of sad. The reason we had come to get something to eat, I think, was so Sidewinder could tell me goodbye.

"When Zack calls for a new deck and the box it's in is blue, you're going to catch a pat hand. Everybody else in the game is going to have hands that will keep the raises going, to help bid you up. I don't know what your hand'll be; it might even be a straight flush, but it's a cold deck and they'll know their hand is higher, so their last raise will be for everything both us and them have got. You'll make or call the bet, and I'll make sure they're tapped out with another $10,000 on the side. Look for a $30,000 to $40,000 pot unless they don't call the last bet, but don't worry, no matter what it is you've got, it's going to be the winner."

And from there, your honor, it's not hard to figure out what had happened. Percy had told Sidewinder how the Luster brothers operated, like I told you earlier, and put together the decks Sidewinder needed. Sidewinder had gotten Jimmy D. to pose as a beer delivery man to get him into the club to set things up on the inside. My guess is, he found out where Shaw kept the cold decks, and planted the fake fakes.

When we got back to the table, your honor, they were waiting for us, and the room was darker than I had noticed it being. It was also the first time I noticed that the Luster brothers both had mustaches, and I remember thinking how I would hate being killed before I'd gotten to see my own mustache grown full out and waxed at least once.

Sidewinder had another trick up his sleeve that he me about. He reached over, spread the chips out on the table in front of me, and made the club turn them back into real cash, right there in the open in front of all the witnesses. When we had the $6,000 in cash in front of us, Sidewinder then told them, "There's what we have to play with, plus this," and he showed $10,000 more, which he had in his pocket, and said, "Now let's all either play for cash or call it quits."

They had to come up with the cash or nobody would have trusted their chips ever again and they'd be out of business. It took them a while, and I think they had to borrow some money from the big safe in the Lodge office, but they got it up.

"Straight poker," Zack said, and he snapped his fingers and called for a new deck. Shaw brought it and it was blue. Zack opened the box and took out the new cards. He shuffled them twice, pulled them through, and handed them to the stooge on his right. The stooge didn't even cut—just tapped the top of the deck with his finger like people sometimes do, and said, "Go ahead and deal, I trust you."

The ante was $100 and the opening bid was $500 more. By the time it came to me it was already up to $1,100 and I looked at my cards for the first time. I was holding four sevens and a nine, and so I raised.

"Let's play for $2,500," I said, and threw in $1,400. From there it was call-call-call and cards. It didn't hurt me to throw away the nine and take one card. Three people in the game each took one card, and three stayed pat.

I knew I wasn't going to lose, and so it wasn't anything like real poker. In a way, though, it was worse because my hands were sweating and my throat was dry and I was so scared I could taste the air. Everybody was counting out $100 bills and throwing them in the pot. When the betting came next around to me, I did what I was supposed to do with a natural four of a kind, and raised my last $1,000, which cleaned me out.

"Plus $10,000 more," Sidewinder said, and threw the pile he had in the middle.

That was all the Luster brothers had, and all they wanted, so one of us was going to be wiped out, and Harvey, who was supposed to win, just called. He had four sixes, and was about to reach out and drag the pot when I showed him the sevens. The next thing I know for sure, Zack had hit me across the mouth with something heavy, the barrel of his gun, I think, and caved my teeth in. A flashbulb went off in my eyes—Randall had taken the picture you saw in court, the one with me flying backwards— and my blood flying everywhere. (The dentist says I might have to wear the braces on my teeth for another two years, so you know how hard he hit me.)

And now here is the rest of it. I was on the floor. I felt like I was blind from the flashbulb, and had cotton in my ears from the rap in the face, and all I could hear was guns going off—10 shots, 12 shots, I don't have any way of knowing. They say the gunfight at the old O.K. Corral only took 30 seconds. I'll bet the one at the new O.K. Corral that I was in didn't take half that long. I was trying to get up, but somebody fell across me and I couldn't see, hear, or breathe, and it was Sidewinder, and he was dead. I knew that from the way he felt when I felt his face, and I remember feeling glad it was over. Except it wasn't over, as you know.

The last person standing was Jimmy D., and then he fell over, too. They said in court that he had been shot six times in all, and from three different sides, so it makes me think that he shot Zack and Jim Pat first, because they were shot between the eyes, which was where Jimmy D. liked to aim. Then I think Harvey and Swifty and Shaw all put bullets in him. I think he got Swifty with his last shot and just stood there till he fell. I think Sidewinder and Harvey both kind of got each other, and Shaw was the only one still living when I got Sidewinder off of me and got up. I don't even know how the gun got in my hand, your honor, but there it was, and when Shaw brought his gun up and tried to shoot me, I shot him instead.

The money was still there in the pot. A person doesn't think straight in those kinds of situations, and all I could think about was that it belonged to us. I was shaking, and scared, and trying to get it all folded into small rolls and was stuffing it into Sidewinder's coat pockets. It was Randall who came over and made me stop and sat me down at the table, and that's where I was when Sheriff Paul Buchanan came and arrested me.

And now it's late Monday afternoon, and I have told you my side of the story, and Mr. Harmon is coming first thing in the morning to pick this all up. It makes me feel funny to be done with it all. I keep trying to think through everything I've said, trying to think of things I've left out that might be important.

Tuesday morning, November 2, 1948

Dear Judge, your honor,

I got up extra early to write this, but it will still have to be quick because, like I told you, Mr. Harmon is coming for it, and is going to be here, he said, when the jail opens.

This might be the last chance I have to talk to you about my case as you will be sentencing me on Friday, and there is still something I need to tell you. It is how I feel about what all happened. Mr. Harmon, my lawyer, says I should tell you that I'm sorry I did it, but I'm not sure I am.

I know I'm not sorry I killed Shaw because he would surely have killed me, and I did not want to die.

And Mr. Harmon says I should say that they pulled their guns first, but I don't know who went for their guns first. I do know this, however: If I couldn't see what was going on because of that flashbulb, neither could any of the so-called witnesses. By the time I quit seeing a big white spot in my eyes, the gunfight was damn well all over. The only ones still in it were me and Shaw.

So, in other words, all those so-called witnesses were trying to do was make themselves seem more important than they were.

That made me mad at the trial, but it doesn't bother me

now because it's what people always do when they start telling stories.

Jimmy D. is still pretty much a mystery to me, and I keep wondering what kind of person he really was. I think I know sometimes, but I still can't understand it. Jimmy D. just didn't take any sass from anybody. And sometimes you've got to be that way.

I don't have much longer and I'm trying to think of everything I can. . . .

I can't think of nothing, so I guess that's just plain it. It's been my pleasure to write all of this stuff down because it's helped me get it off my chest and given me something to do for the last few weeks.

I wish you could have known Sidewinder and Jimmy D. because I think you would have liked them.

What else. . . .

How about this: Please don't send me to prison because I *do not want to go.* Sentence me to quit gambling till I'm 21 and I guarantee you, cross my heart, that it shall be done. Sentence me to get out of Arkansas and that shall be done, too, quicker than you can probably blink your eyes.

I've been thinking about that a lot lately—where I'd go if you did, and I keep coming up with the same picture. It's sometime in the future, but I'm not a whole lot older. I'm on a desert island; there's sand and the ocean and coconut trees and a hammock, and I'm wearing a grass skirt and everything.

And I know what it is, your honor, it's that nightclub act I saw in Memphis, but this time the picture has me in it, and I'm the one who's the King of Bongo-Bong.

Let me go, your honor, and I promise you I'll send you a postcard.

Mr. Harmon, my lawyer, is here and ready for me to

give this up, and so I will say goodbye until I have a new address. Ha-ha. Here's hoping it's Bongo-Bong and not you-know-where.

Yours truly,
Dumas Monk

OTTO R. SALASSI was born in Vicksburg, Mississippi—home of Dumas Monk himself! A teacher and writer by profession, he has written several other critically acclaimed novels for young adults, including *On the Ropes* and *And Nobody Knew They Were There*. He now lives in Fayetteville, Arkansas.

When the world's at war,
there's no such thing as innocent fun...

THE MACHINE GUNNERS
by Robert Westall

Chas McGill, who's already got a fair-size collection of scavenged World War II souvenirs, has just found the greatest prize of his young life. It's a machine gun, still attached to a Nazi fighter plane downed in the woods of northern England. Enlisting the help of his closest friends, Chas hides the gun from the prying eyes of safety-minded adults—who soon notice that it's disappeared—by building a secret bunker around it. As the local authorities mount a search for the lethal weapon, Chas and company have their own agenda to attend to. There are rumors of an imminent German invasion, and guess who plans to be prepared with a carefully orchestrated counterattack—and the perfect weapon?

"The best book so far written for children about the Second World War."

—*The Times* (London)

"A bloody good story! A well characterized and suspenseful portrayal of the destructiveness of children's war games modelled on adult behavior."

—*School Library Journal*

Winner of the Carnegie Medal
A Boston Globe–Horn Book Honor Book
A Child Study Association of America Children's
Book of the Year

A BORZOI SPRINTER PUBLISHED BY ALFRED A. KNOPF, INC.

ROBIN F. BRANCATO

is..."One of juvenile fiction's best authors!"
—*The Philadelphia Inquirer*

UNEASY MONEY

When Mike Bronti buys himself a lottery ticket to celebrate his 18th birthday, he winds up with a gift of a lifetime—two and a half million dollars! Too bad reality has to set in and ruin a perfectly good dream come true. First, Mike starts acting cocky, especially in front of his father, who's having his own money troubles and is beginning to resent Mike's good luck. And things *really* blow up in his face when he announces—on TV, no less!—the formation of his own personal charity fund. Suddenly everyone wants a piece of the action! Can he buy back his old way of life, Mike wonders desperately? Can he afford not to?

An IRA Young Adults' Choice

WINNING

A week ago he was "superjock" senior Gary Madden, hero of the high school football team with prospects as limitless as his own imagination. Now he lies in a hospital bed, the victim of a freak accident that's left him completely paralyzed. Overwhelmed by the flood of good wishes and kind advice from friends and family, one question continues to haunt him. Is life as "Superquad," the all-star patient, really worth it?

An ALA Best Book for Young Adults
A Library of Congress Children's Book of the Year

BORZOI SPRINTERS PUBLISHED BY ALFRED A. KNOPF, INC.

PHILIP PULLMAN

"is a master of atmosphere and style"
—*School Library Journal*

THE RUBY IN THE SMOKE

"Beware the seven blessings..." When sixteen-year-old Sally Lockhart utters these words, an employee of her late father dies of fear. And thus begins her terrifying journey into the seamy underworld of Victorian London, in search of clues that will solve the puzzle of her father's death. Pursued by villains and cutthroats at every turn, she at last uncovers two dark mysteries. Sally soon learns that she is the key to both—and that it's worth her very life to find out why.

**Winner of the International Reading Association's
Children's Book Award
An ALA Best Book for Young Adults**

SHADOW IN THE NORTH

It's six years later, and Sally is now a financial consultant in London. But when one of her clients loses a fortune on the strength of her advice, she's determined to recover the money. Soon Sally, her paramour Frederick, and their friend Jim are hot on the trail of Axel Bellmann, a wealthy, unscrupulous businessman. What they uncover is a plot so diabolical that it could eventually subvert the entire civilized world—and if Bellmann has his way, Sally and her friends won't even live long enough to see it happen!

**An ALA Best Book for Young Adults
A *Booklist* Editors' Choice
Nominated for the Edgar Allan Poe Award for Best Mystery**

BORZOI SPRINTERS PUBLISHED BY ALFRED A. KNOPF, INC.